D0325332

SWEET PROMISES

A CANDLE BEACH SWEET ROMANCE

NICOLE ELLIS

Copyright © 2017 by Nicole Ellis

All rights reserved.

No part of this book may be reproduced in any form or by any electronic
or mechanical means, including information storage and retrieval systems,
without written permission from the author, except for the use of brief
quotations in a book review.

Cover art by: RL Sathers/SelfPubBookCovers.com

Cover typography by: Mariah Sinclair

Editing by: Free Bird Editing —

Serena Clarke and LaVerne Clark

❀ Created with Vellum

"*A*lbert, I need those turkeys by Wednesday." Maggie Price leaned back in the chair with the phone pressed to her ear and tapped a pen against the wooden desk. The phone beeped insistently to alert her to another call. Whoever it was would have to wait. This call with her supplier was too important to interrupt.

"Look, I'm sorry, but there's nothing I can do about it." The man on the other end of the phone call sighed. "You're not going to have them by Thanksgiving. I might be able to get you something else, but with that storm dumping snow in Portland, there's no way that we'll be able to get the turkeys to you in time. Nothing's getting through."

"I'll see if I can get someone else to deliver them," she said. "I'll talk to you tomorrow, okay?"

"Maggie, you know I'd get them for you if I could, but my hands are tied. I'm sorry." He sighed again.

"I know. Thanks for trying." She hung up the phone and stared at the ceiling in her tiny office. Although no cobwebs hung from the corners, the paint had worn thin in places and the office showed its age. When she'd bought the

Greasy Spoon from the former owner and revamped it into the Bluebonnet Café, she'd put all her money and efforts into the customer-facing portions of the café and kitchen, leaving no spare cash for anything behind the scenes. She shook her head. There were bigger problems at the moment than scratched paint.

What was she going to do with no turkeys to serve for Thanksgiving dinner at the café? There'd be a rebellion in Candle Beach. Many of the townspeople didn't have relatives close by and they counted on having their holiday dinner at her restaurant. She stared blankly at the computer screen, which showed her order for the turkeys that wouldn't be arriving any time soon.

Someone knocked on the door. She regarded it wearily. What now?

"Come in."

"Maggie?" Her lead waitress, Belinda, pushed the door open, sending the aroma of freshly baked apple pies throughout the office. Maggie's stomach grumbled. Lunch had been hours ago. She pasted an 'everything's alright' smile on her face for her employee's benefit.

"What's going on?"

"It's your mom. She said she can't watch Alex any longer today—she's got to get to work." Belinda looked apologetic. "She said you were supposed to be there an hour ago."

Maggie shot a glance at the old-fashioned analog clock on the wall and jumped out of her chair. Dealing with the supply snafu had taken longer than she'd thought.

"It's six thirty already? Is she still on the phone?"

"Yeah, I put her on hold," Belinda said. "You've been in here since I started my dinner shift at five. Is everything okay?"

"Things are fine. Can you please tell her I'll be there in

less than ten minutes?" She threw on her winter jacket and rushed past Belinda. "Thanks!"

"Sure, I'll let her know," Belinda called after her.

Everything was not okay. A winter storm south of them in Oregon had ground all of her suppliers' trucks to a halt. She'd been trying to improvise on their daily menu, but something had to give. She'd even had to send someone to the local grocery store to scrounge for hamburger buns that morning. The way it was going, they'd be having Spam and frozen peas for Thanksgiving dinner in two days. That would not go over well with her regulars.

The big holiday meals were always a pain to coordinate, but people in town who didn't have family or friends nearby appreciated her having the café open for them to eat at. She knew most of the people in this small town, either through the café or from growing up there, and she didn't want to let anyone down.

She drove the mile to her parents' house, her mind spinning with everything she needed to take care of. Juggling the schedule for the café and care for her six-year-old son, Alex, was a constant struggle. In a few weeks, he'd be off school for winter break and things would become even more complicated. She wasn't looking forward to that. As soon as she reached her parents' house, she parked crookedly in an empty parking spot and ran inside.

～

"Thank goodness you're here," Charlene Johansen, Maggie's mom, said. "I've got to get to work at the market. I was supposed to be there thirty minutes ago."

"I'm sorry, Mom. I totally lost track of time. Things have been crazy at the café." Maggie felt horrible about being late. Having her mom babysit Alex was a lifesaver and she couldn't get along without her.

"It's okay, honey. One of my co-workers is covering for me, but I need to get there soon. Dad had to work late, or I'd have him take Alex." She searched her daughter's face. "What's going on?"

"Nothing, everything is fine."

"Really? Because you don't look so good."

Maggie opened her mouth to reply, but Alex came barreling around the corner. "Mommy! You have to see the new Lego set Grandma bought me. It's Minecraft!"

"Mom...you bought him more Legos?" She narrowed her eyes at her mother.

Charlene blushed. "He had the first of the two sets, so I bought him the second. He's my only grandchild. Let me spoil him a little." She kissed the top of Alex's head and patted her daughter's hand. "I've got to go. Lock up when you leave."

"Bye. Have fun at work." Maggie called to her. Then she turned to Alex. "C'mon, kiddo. Let's get home and you can show me your new Legos while I make dinner." He ran off to the family room to get his toys and she leaned against the open door to wait for him.

"Got 'em." He pushed past her and she locked the door behind them. He ran ahead of her out to the driveway, opened the car door and got into his booster seat. Maggie sat in the driver's seat and stared at her son in the rearview mirror. Her husband Brian would have been amazed to see how much Alex had grown over the last five years. Brian had been an Army soldier. He died in the Middle East when Alex was a baby and never had the chance to see what a wonderful little person his son had become.

She put the car in reverse and drove home to the tiny

two-bedroom apartment she shared with Alex. Candle Beach didn't have much in the way of large apartment complexes like in the big city, but she'd been lucky to find a place in a fourplex less than a mile from the café.

After admiring Alex's new Lego set, feeding him and getting him to bed, she was bushed. She grabbed her planning notebook and flopped on the couch, covering her legs with a lightweight afghan. She flipped on the TV while she worked on an updated menu for the café's Thanksgiving dinner. The TV provided background noise but she barely heard it.

The unsettled feeling she'd had all day kept nagging at her. She'd made the Bluebonnet Café a success, but she wanted something more. She'd volunteered to cater her friend Dahlia's wedding to test out a new catering business, hoping that it would fulfill her Type A personality's desire for a new challenge. And challenging it had been.

Running the café, starting a new catering business, and being a single mother wasn't easy. Would she be able to do it all? She dropped her head to the pillowy couch arm and closed her eyes. Things would work out. She'd always found a way to get everything done in the past.

~

The next morning, Maggie dropped Alex off at school and headed for the cafe. Only one day remained before Thanksgiving and she still didn't have a main course for the big holiday meal. She called every supplier in her notebook, but understandably, they were either sold out of turkeys at such late notice, or they had the same problem with the snow as her original supplier. Finally, after a few hours, she procured some hams that a supplier assured her would get there by the next day. They weren't what her customers would expect for Thanksgiving, but they'd have to do.

With that crisis averted, she finished planning the rest of the menu. Thank goodness they had potatoes. If there were no mashed potatoes as well as no turkey, there would be a riot for sure.

Her best pastry chef and right-hand woman, Bernadette, stuck her head past the half-opened door. "Maggie? Do you have time?"

"Time for what?" Maggie set down her notebook. "If there's something wrong with the latest food shipment, I don't want to hear about it." She smiled to let her employee know she was kidding.

"No, no. Nothing like that." Bernadette grinned and approached her desk. "I'm scheduled to work on Friday, but my boyfriend invited me to go away for the weekend. Lily said she'd take my shift in the kitchen. Is that okay with you?"

Phew. Nothing major. She didn't think she could take anything else.

"Of course, go ahead. I hope you have fun." Lily wasn't as hard of a worker as Bernadette, but business should be slow on the Friday after Thanksgiving.

"Thanks!" Bernadette turned and sailed out of the room.

Maggie thought about starting in on the schedule for the week after next, but a quick glance at her watch changed her mind. Alex had a half day at school and she needed to pick him up soon.

"I'll be back after five," she called to her kitchen staff. They waved to show they'd heard, but continued working on orders from the lunch rush.

≈

After she got Alex home, he ran off to his room to play and she collapsed on the couch. Her split shift days were exhausting. She always intended to rest on the couch while at home, but household chores or other projects tended to grab her attention. Today was no different. She'd stacked her supplies for Dahlia's bridal shower decorations and party favors in the corner, and the half-finished boxes for the petit fours mocked her.

She sighed. At least if she got them done today, there would be less to do on Friday night. She flipped on the TV and mindlessly watched an old Friends episode while folding the small boxes. She'd ordered the boxes and lids from a craft supply store in Haven Shores, but it hadn't occurred to her how much time it would take to assemble them. Gretchen had volunteered to help with the party favors, but she'd told her not to worry. In hindsight, she probably should have accepted the help.

Making the petit fours should be fun though. Before she'd had Alex, she'd been a bored Army wife, living in a community far away from all of her friends and family, with the exception of Brian. At their last duty station, she'd taken pastry-making and cake-decorating classes at the local culinary school. Now, other than the desserts she helped make for the café, she didn't have much call to make fancy cakes. She'd searched YouTube and found a 'how to' video for making petit fours. She planned to place four in each of the paper boxes. Then she'd wrap a ribbon around the outside and tie it neatly with a bow. She brightened. The final product would be worth it and the guests would love them.

By the time she needed to take Alex to her parents' house for the evening, she had finished forming the boxes, but there was still a long list of things to do for the shower. Tomorrow was Thanksgiving, and after she worked a morning shift, she and Alex would go to her parents' house for dinner. That left Friday. She eyed the pile of decorations. Yeah, plenty of time.

She brushed off her hands and called down the hallway. "Alex! Time to go."

"Do I have to?" he whined.

"Yes. Sorry buddy, but you're only six. I can't leave you home alone and I have to work."

"But Dylan's mom stays home with him. He gets to stay at home and play all day after school and not go anywhere else."

Maggie mentally counted to ten. "Well, I have to work. Now get your shoes on."

He grumbled more at her, but reluctantly did as he was told. At times like this, Maggie really wished she had a partner to help parent Alex. Being the sole provider and caregiver for her little family was stressful, and having someone else to share things with would make life much easier. Her parents were a big help, but it wasn't the same as having her husband home to help. She hadn't dated anyone since Brian and she wasn't sure if she wanted to, so gaining a partner was a far-off dream.

If business continued to do well at the café, she might be able to afford a house cleaner or a full-time nanny soon. That would help, but it wouldn't be the same as having someone to share everything with. *If wishes were horses*, she thought. She wasn't sure what it meant, but her mother said it often and it seemed appropriate for her current situation.

"I'm ready." Alex yanked the door open and sprinted out to the car, waiting impatiently for her to unlock it.

She beeped it from the front porch. At five o'clock, the sky had already darkened. The short days of winter were rough and she wished for some summer sun to brighten her day. At least winter meant the holidays, and after Thanksgiving was over, she was free to put up the Christmas tree and decorate with lights. Christmas was her favorite time of year. There was something enchanting about seeing lights adorning buildings and hearing Santa Claus ringing the bell for the Salvation Army outside the grocery store. Sometimes, it even snowed in Candle Beach, although being on the ocean, they didn't usually get much accumulation.

This year would be extra special with Dahlia's wedding a week before Christmas. Not only was she catering the wedding, but she and another friend, Gretchen, were Dahlia's only bridesmaids. She pulled her coat closed and hurried to the car. There was so much to do—all the bridal shower and catering prep for Dahlia's wedding, the holiday decorating, and she still needed to buy a few stocking stuffers for Alex. She took a deep breath to calm herself and opened the car door, ready to receive another tongue lashing from her sixteen-year-old in a six-year-old's body.

2

_J_ake Price knocked most of the snow off of his winter boots, then removed them and set them outside the door of his parents' house. Portland, Oregon, had been hit unusually hard by a recent snowstorm and the historic Craftsman homes on the block looked like a Norman Rockwell winter scene. He didn't bother to knock before entering.

The telltale scent of a turkey roasting in the oven tantalized his senses as soon as he pushed the door open. His mother's voice led him to the kitchen, where she perched on a barstool with her back to him, talking to someone on the phone.

"We'll still see you for Christmas, right?" Barbara Price slumped slightly at whatever the caller said. "Only for two days? Can Alex stay longer?"

Jake could hear the disappointment in her voice.

"Okay, honey, we'll talk to you later." She set the phone on the counter and slid off the stool, resting against the bar.

"Mom," he said.

She put her hand to her chest and spun around to face him. "Don't sneak up on me like that. I'm an old woman."

"Not so old," he said, coming up to her and wrapping his arms around her shoulders. She returned the hug and scrutinized him.

"Did you come by to do laundry? Thanksgiving dinner doesn't start until one o'clock." She glanced at the clock. "It's only ten."

"No," he laughed. "I came by to give you a hand." He grabbed a red-and-green apron from a hook on the wall. "What can I do? Put me to work."

She beamed. "You can peel and quarter the potatoes. Your father usually does it, but I sent him to the store for butter." She shook her head. "I forgot to add it to the grocery list when he went to the market yesterday. Ah, I'm getting old." She rolled out a mound of dough sitting on the floured counter.

Jake tied the apron strings around his waist and sat down across from her at the bar. The potato peeler felt tiny in his large hands, but he quickly got the hang of it. He peeled a few potatoes and then asked, "Was that Maggie you were talking to? She's not coming to Thanksgiving this year? I'd hoped to see her. It's been a long time since we both came to a holiday meal."

His mother's smile slipped. "No, she's in charge of the restaurant today. She and Alex will come down to Portland for a few days at the end of December."

"But not for as much time as you'd like to see Alex, right?"

"Maggie's really busy. She'll bring him down here when she can. That girl has a lot on her plate." She hesitated. "She sounded more stressed than I've ever heard her. I wish I could go up there and help out with Alex, but I've got my job at the library. I think she may have bitten off more than she can chew this time. You know Maggie."

She busied herself preparing the lattice crust for an apple pie, but concern was etched across her face.

He did know Maggie, enough to know she was the most driven woman he'd ever met. When his younger brother Brian brought her home at his college's Christmas break to meet the family the first time, she'd mapped out every minute of her time in Portland, determined to make the most of it. They'd affectionately called her 'Maggie the human dynamo' behind her back. Brian had been smitten from the moment he met her, and they got married in the December following his college graduation.

Jake had been stationed with the Army at Fort Lewis, Washington, at the time and had been able to get home for their wedding. Soon after they married, Brian had left for his Officer Basic Course in Missouri, taking Maggie with him.

A portrait of his brother in uniform sat on the mantel, drawing his attention. He and his parents had been devastated when Brian was killed in the Middle East and he couldn't imagine how Maggie had felt, especially with a little baby.

Before Brian deployed for the Middle East, his parents had hosted a family picnic in their backyard. He remembered it had been a bright, sunny summer day. A perfect kind of day, where nothing bad could happen. Maggie had worn a white sundress imprinted with red roses and carried Alex in a wrap around her front. He'd watched as Brian wrapped an arm around his wife and kissed his son on the forehead. His love for his family shone through in his actions and Jake had wondered if he himself would ever experience the same happiness.

After a neighbor drew Maggie into conversation, his brother had taken him aside and made him promise to take care of Maggie and Alex if something should happen to him. Jake had slugged him on the shoulder.

"You'll be fine, little bro. Nothing's going to happen to you." Jake had been on two tours to the Middle East himself and knew things weren't great over there, but he didn't want his brother to worry about leaving his wife and child behind.

"I know, but just the same, promise me you'll do this for me?" Brian had smiled, but his lips quivered as he patted Jake on the back. It was the last time they saw each other before Brian headed overseas.

When Brian didn't make it back, Jake intended to make good on his promise, but the Army had other ideas and stationed him in Korea for three years and then Germany for two. He'd kept up with Maggie and Alex's lives through phone calls with his mother and he sent birthday cards to Alex, but his involvement hadn't extended past that. The years passed faster than he'd realized. After twenty years in the Army, he'd recently opted for retirement. Now here he was, back in the States, retired at the ripe old age of thirty-eight.

He gazed out the window at the empty snow-covered lawn, so different than his memory of the warm summer backyard picnic so many years ago. He returned his attention to his mother.

"I could go help with Alex for a few weeks."

"You?" She scoffed. "What do you know about kids?"

He shrugged. "I'll manage. I've been around kids before, you know."

Her demeanor softened. "What about your Border Patrol interview?"

"I'll head up there after my interview on Monday. I'm sure they won't call me back for a while. The federal government moves at the speed of a snail with their hiring process. I'd like to see Alex, and Maggie too, of course. It's been years since I saw him." He thought for a moment and counted the years. His brother had already been gone for five years? Alex would be about six now.

"Well, I'm sure Alex will be happy to see you. From what Maggie says, he'd love to have a man around. He's been wanting to play catch with someone and begging her to enroll him in Little League. Can you imagine Maggie playing softball?"

He could actually. He had a feeling his sister-in-law could do anything she set her mind to. But how would he do with a six-year-old? He'd spent time with the kids of an ex-girlfriend when they'd been dating, but it wasn't the same as with family. And that had been years ago. His ex hadn't been able to handle a long-distance relationship and they'd amicably broken up soon after he moved to Korea. He'd heard from friends that she was now happily married to a local guy.

"I have a few things to wrap up here, but I'll leave on Tuesday for Candle Beach. Don't say anything to Maggie though, okay? I want to surprise her and Alex."

His mother looked relieved. "I'm sure she'd welcome your help."

He wasn't convinced of that, but he knew he had to offer. He owed his brother that much.

"I can't wait until I retire. Only three years to go. Then I can visit Alex whenever I want. And maybe in a few years I'll have more grandkids...hint, hint." She eyed him.

He sighed. "When I can find a woman to stick with me. I haven't had much luck so far."

She patted him on the arm. "You'll find someone. You're a good man. The right woman is out there for you."

"Maybe." He was pushing forty. If he hadn't found the right woman yet, what were the odds he'd find her anytime soon? He'd had his share of romantic relationships, but most of them had been short-lived. Some due to the natural fizzling out of things, but most because of Army commitments. But the Army wasn't part of his life anymore, so now it was all on him. That thought both exhilarated and terrified him.

~

After he watched the football game with his dad and helped his mom clean up the dishes, Jake went back to the extended-stay hotel room he'd lived in for the past month. It smelled like lemon cleaning solution, a sharp contrast to the homey aroma of turkey and apple pie that had pervaded his parents' house. He'd stayed at the hotel to maintain his independence, but this definitely wasn't home.

If he planned to visit Maggie and Alex for a week or more, he'd need to clean out his hotel room. No point in paying for a room he wasn't using. He glanced around.

His application materials for the US Border Patrol sat on a desk pushed against the wall. Was that where his future lay? He'd enlisted as a teenager and the Army had been his life up until now. Other than his decision to attend college and commission as an officer through the Green to Gold program, he hadn't had to make many career decisions. Now that he had the chance to be around family, did he really want to move up to the Canadian border, away from everyone he knew and loved?

He turned his gaze to his belongings. He planned to

pack everything and be ready to drive up to Candle Beach right after his interview.

It wouldn't take him long. After twenty years of military moves, he hadn't accumulated much stuff. Most of it was in a local storage unit. The hotel room was as austere and uninviting as it had been when he'd moved in. Being in the Army didn't make building anything easy, whether it be a romantic relationship or a sense of home. Now that he was officially a civilian, he intended to make the most of it. Visiting his nephew in Candle Beach might be exactly what he needed to start out his new life.

3

*D*ealing with employees wasn't any more fun than dealing with a young child. There had been some grumbling by customers and employees about the lack of Thanksgiving turkey, but the hams had been well-received and Maggie and Alex had spent a nice, relaxing Thanksgiving dinner with her parents. Now, however, it was back to real life at the café.

"You can't book parties that large for the side room." Velma James stared at Maggie with her hands firmly planted on her ample hips. They stood just inside the stockroom behind the front counter, where Maggie could still monitor everything happening inside the café.

She closed her eyes. She'd just informed Velma that the party room had been reserved for that evening. This wasn't the first time her employee had given her grief for having so many people in their side room. The woman had been around since the Bluebonnet Café was the Greasy Spoon and was one of the few people she couldn't get along with.

Velma was a member of the Ladies of Candle Beach Club and Maggie had no idea how old she was. The older woman had a history of arguing with customers and messing up orders. She probably should have been fired years ago, but Maggie didn't have the heart to do so. It couldn't be easy for an elderly woman to find a job in Candle Beach—not with her temperament.

"It's all we have," Maggie said in a steely voice. "If we don't take the booking, they'll go to Haven Shores instead."

"Well, maybe they should," Velma said stubbornly. "Why, I can barely squeeze past the person at the end to bring the guests on the other side of the table their entrees."

One, two, three... Maggie counted to ten slowly—the same technique she used when dealing with Alex. Velma wasn't going to get the best of her. The day had been too long to lose her cool over the woman's silly antics.

"The party room has a maximum capacity of thirty people. We're well under that."

"Yes, but with the serving cart and all those chairs in there, it's ridiculously cramped."

"Velma," Maggie said sharply. "I'm doing my best. Please go make up the salads for table six. They've been waiting quite a while for them." She stared pointedly over at the table she'd referenced, where the guests were doing the telltale head dart as they searched for their absent waitress.

"Fine, but when a guest gets soup spilled on their lap because there wasn't enough room to get around them, don't say I didn't tell you so." Velma flounced off in her white tennis shoes.

For all her lack of charm and grace, Velma had a point. With the growing local and tourist population in Candle Beach, her party room was rapidly becoming too small to meet demand. In fact, last week she'd had to turn down a family reunion because she couldn't fit fifty people into that room and the adjoining main room wasn't conducive to housing large get-togethers.

What could she do though? Her fledgling catering business was just starting to get off the ground. Dahlia was her first big customer, but there had been a few other small gigs as well that had come up in the last month. To grow any bigger, she'd need to locate an events venue that could house at least one hundred people, if not more. But where was she going to find that? To the best of her knowledge, Candle Beach didn't have such a thing. The closest thing would be to rent out the wine bar, but they probably wouldn't want their whole establishment closed for a day any more than she wanted to do so with the café.

She added finding a venue to the running to-do list she had in her planner and reviewed her checklist for Dahlia's bridal shower one last time. She needed to make the petit fours and finish some decorations. Should be a piece of cake.

~

The preparations for Dahlia's bridal shower turned out to be anything but a piece of cake. Everything seemed to take four times as long as she'd expected. After she made it through the Thanksgiving turkey fiasco unscathed, Maggie had turned all of her attention to the shower. She and Gretchen had planned a tea party theme and had collected tea pots from friends and family over the last month in anticipation of the event.

Gretchen's tenant, their friend Charlotte, had recently moved out of Gretchen's house when an apartment in town opened up, allowing Gretchen to move back in and host the event. In return, Maggie had said she'd provide all the food and decorations. It had turned out to be much more time intensive than she'd thought it would be.

"Maggie." Gretchen placed a doily on an end table and stared at her friend. "Are you okay?"

Maggie yawned and waved her hand. "I'm fine. Those party favors took quite a bit of time. Who'd have thought making twenty boxes of petit fours would take so long?"

Gretchen eyed the perfectly packed boxes. "Uh, I would. Did you make those yourself?"

Maggie regarded her with surprise. "Of course. I watched a YouTube video on how to make them. They're similar to something I studied in a cake-decorating class series. But I couldn't get them quite right at first." She yawned again.

"What time did you go to bed last night?" Gretchen asked.

"Around three, but then Alex was up at six. I couldn't manage to talk him into watching cartoons while I slept, so I got up and made pancakes."

"Mags, you're crazy. You need to get more sleep. I would have helped with the party favors, but you said they were simple to do."

Maggie frowned. "They shouldn't have taken that long. I don't know why it took me so long to learn how to make them."

Gretchen shook her head and smiled. "Why don't you come sit down over here to rest? Dahlia and the guests won't be here for a while longer."

"Maybe just for a minute." The couch in Gretchen's living room did look inviting. She fell asleep as soon as her head hit the soft upholstery.

She didn't wake up until the doorbell rang. She flew up

from the couch and ran to the kitchen where Gretchen stood heating water at the stove.

"Why didn't you wake me up? There's so much to do." Her eyes darted around the kitchen frantically.

"Relax. I've got it covered. You needed to sleep." Gretchen pointed to teapots full of steeping tea and trays of neatly arranged scones and tea sandwiches. "I put the scones next to the clotted cream and jam you brought over."

"But I should have been helping." Anxiety rose up inside of her, causing her heart rate to increase.

"You made all the scones and the party favors. I think you've done plenty." Gretchen's eyes drilled into her face. "You need to slow down a bit. Remember when I was so sick from all the stress a few months ago? You told me to take it easy. Now I'm giving your own advice right back to you."

The doorbell rang again and their guests knocked on the door.

She knew Gretchen was right. With the Thanksgiving turkey issues at the restaurant and then the bridal shower preparations right on its heels, she hadn't been taking very good care of herself. But between work and Alex, there just wasn't enough time for her too. "I'm fine." She smiled. "Now, we should probably let the guests in."

They laughed and hurried into the front room to open the door.

"Are we early?" Dahlia's future mother-in-law Wendy asked, looking around the room. "I started to worry we were at the wrong place."

Dahlia peeked out from behind her and rolled her eyes. "I told her this was Gretchen's house."

Maggie smiled. "No, sorry about that. We were back in the kitchen. Come on in." From what Dahlia had said, she was surprised to see Wendy was the first guest. She was more known for her free-spiritedness than her punctuality. It must have been due to the positive influence of her new husband, a local accountant.

"Dahlia, you look gorgeous," Gretchen said. Their friend wore a long-sleeved purple dress with a flared skirt and low heels. Dahlia spun in a full circle to show them the colorful inside pleats of the dress.

"Thank you. I found this dress in Seattle when Garrett and I visited my parents last month."

"Is your mom here?" Maggie asked. Vanessa, Dahlia's mother, had RSVP'd but said she might be late as she would be leaving straight from an important business meeting in Seattle.

"She just called and said she was about thirty minutes out of town."

Dahlia wandered into the kitchen and then turned back to them. "Maggie, Gretchen, this is beautiful." She gave them both huge hugs. "Thanks, you guys. I really appreciate this."

"Of course," Maggie said. "It was our pleasure." She and Gretchen exchanged pleased glances.

A few more guests arrived, including Bernadette and Sandy, who were both waitresses at the Bluebonnet Café. Dahlia had only been in town for a year and a half, but she'd quickly made friends.

"Hi Bernadette, Sandy. Glad you could make it." Maggie took their coats and motioned to the kitchen. "Help yourselves to a cup of tea." She took all the coats she'd collected upstairs and laid them on the bed in the guest room. Outside, the sky was gray and the ocean churned in choppy whitecaps from the wintry gusts of wind.

She came downstairs to find everyone gathered around Bernadette, oohing and aahing.

"What's going on?" She approached the group and saw the glittery stone on Bernadette's left hand.

"Lee asked me to marry him." Bernadette flashed the ring at her boss.

Maggie hugged her. "Congratulations! Why didn't you say anything earlier?"

"I didn't want to intrude on Dahlia's special day, but they saw the ring." She glowed with happiness.

"And they're moving to a small town in Alaska," another guest piped up. "Isn't that so romantic?"

Maggie's heart sank. Her best employee was moving to Alaska? Although great for Bernadette, this was horrible for the café.

"Alaska?" She gave Bernadette a quizzical look.

Bernadette looked sheepish. "Yeah, Lee got a job on a fishing boat up there for the summer. I'm going to work in the cannery."

"Ah. So you're not moving until summer."

"No, we're moving soon so we can get settled in a little house up there." She twisted her engagement ring. "I guess this is my official two weeks' notice? I'm so sorry, Maggie. I've loved working for you, but I don't want to be so far apart from Lee. Maybe I can help you find my replacement?"

"Don't worry about it. I'm happy for you and Lee." Maggie hugged her again.

She turned to the other guests, who were chatting in small groups throughout the main floor, raising her voice to be heard over them.

"Thank you all for coming. I think most everyone is here now, so let's get the party started." The guests quieted and looked at her. "There are scones and tea sandwiches in the kitchen, so if you'd like to get something to eat before we start the bridal shower games, please go ahead." The group milled toward the kitchen.

After the guests had been served food, they played some games Gretchen had prepared.

Maggie read off the instructions for one of the games. "Now, here's one with questions about Dahlia that Garrett has answered. Dahlia has to tell us what she thinks Garrett would say about her."

Dahlia groaned loudly, but a smile spread across her face at the mention of her fiancé.

"First," Gretchen read. "What would Garrett say your favorite food is?"

"Pizza." Dahlia rubbed her stomach. "I could eat it every day. Yum."

"Ding, ding, ding. He did say pizza." Gretchen said. "Now let's move on to a harder one. What would Garrett say is your biggest accomplishment?"

Dahlia paused. "Managing To Be Read. When we met, I could barely run a cash register. Now, the bookstore is so busy that I had to hire full-time help even for the winter." Her mother Vanessa who'd arrived about ten minutes earlier, smiled broadly.

"He did say that." Maggie grinned. "And now for an even more difficult question. What is your biggest dream for the future?"

She deliberated on the question. "Hmm."

"That is a tricky one," Gretchen said. "I don't think Parker knows that about me either."

A tear welled in Maggie's eyes before she could think of something happier. Dahlia was engaged and Gretchen was in a solid relationship with her boyfriend, Parker. Would she ever experience a connection with someone again like she had with Brian? Or had her chance at love ended with his death? The dreamy looks she saw in her friends' eyes when they thought about their significant others always made her feel slightly queasy. She pushed the thought out of her mind and brushed her sleeve against her eye. She had Alex and she had to put him first, no matter what. There was little chance that any man could be good enough for both Alex and her.

"You okay?" Charlotte nudged her.

"Yeah, I'm fine. I've got to get something in the kitchen." Maggie stood and picked her way through the crowd of women and went into the kitchen.

She didn't have time to think about men, not if she wanted to accomplish everything she planned to do. Her dreams for the future didn't have room for anyone other than herself and Alex.

4

The drive to Candle Beach was long, but Jake only stopped briefly at a gas station at the midway point. He'd had a few stops to make in Portland before leaving, so by the time he arrived in Candle Beach, it was after eight o'clock. Obeying the speed limit along Main Street slowed his car to a crawl, forcing him to take in the town.

On this Tuesday night in late November, most stores were closed. In the soft glow of the streetlights he could make out a grocery store, a kids clothing store, and a bookstore. A brightly lit grocery store off the main road appeared to be the biggest nightlife in town.

The Bluebonnet Café was still open, but he didn't see many people inside. Was Maggie still at work?

He'd planned to stop by and see her as soon as he reached town, but now he rethought his strategy. Should he wait until the next day to visit? He opted to continue driving the few more blocks to her house. He'd never been to Candle Beach before, but his GPS said he was close to her apartment. He pulled up in front of a fourplex that had been built in the seventies and checked the address his mother had written on a yellow sticky note. This was the place. A light was on in the kitchen. He parked behind a blue Prius and turned off the engine.

Should he knock on the door, or wait until tomorrow? A woman came to the kitchen window, her silhouette outlined by the light behind her. Her lips moved as though she was talking, but there didn't appear to be anyone else in the room. He watched closely and determined she was singing. She turned and he saw her face, with her beautiful features surrounded by curly red hair.

His breath caught. Maggie. The years had treated her well. Small town living must suit her.

He unfolded his cramped legs from his car seat and walked up to her door. He hesitated again before knocking.

She came to the door, but didn't open it. "Who is it?" she asked from behind the safety of the door.

"Jake. Jake Price."

She flung the door open and stared at him with a confused look. "Hi. What are you doing here?" She wore nothing but a thin, pale pink bathrobe and she combed her fingers through still-wet hair, leaving ringlets in their wake. With her face free of makeup, dark circles were apparent under her eyes.

He figured telling her that her mother-in-law thought she needed help wasn't the best approach. "I wanted to come see you and Alex. I had some time off and figured there was no better time than now." He smiled at her and leaned in to awkwardly hug her. His breath caught when he pulled her to him and she seemed to melt against his chest. She smelled like freshly picked roses and the heat from her body made him tingle in a way he wouldn't have expected.

After he released her, she looked flustered. "Alex is in bed." She pulled her pink bathrobe closer against her body.

"I was getting ready for bed myself. I work the morning shift at the Bluebonnet Café."

Of course, he hadn't even thought about that.

"No problem." He smiled again. "I'm staying at a bed and breakfast not too far away. I'll come by tomorrow. What time would work best for you?"

"I'll be home around four. I pick Alex up from my parents' house just before then." She smiled back at him finally, a sweet, soft smile. "I'm sure Alex would love to see you."

She closed the door and he turned to retreat to his car. He stuck his hands in his coat pockets and stopped for a minute to gaze at the sky. Stars shone in the clear night sky, unobscured by stray light like they were in the city. His breath hung in the cold air, but the streets were free of the snow that plagued Portland. In the distance, he heard the faint sound of waves crashing on the shores. He could get used to this.

He turned back to view Maggie's apartment again. She'd turned off the living room light, but he could see another light on at the back of the apartment. She'd obviously not been sleeping enough, and from what his mother had told him, had been taking on too much at work, along with the responsibilities of caring for a child. He should have been there for her like he'd promised Brian. She and Alex needed him.

His interview at the Border Patrol had gone well, but he didn't expect to hear from them for a few more weeks. That would give him enough time to assess the situation with Maggie and Alex and find out what he could do for them. If he got the job, that salary plus his retirement pay from the Army should be more than ample to provide for him and allow for some extras for his sister-in-law—maybe a housekeeper or something that would help lighten the load. He got back into his car and set the GPS for the bed and breakfast he'd arranged to stay at.

~

Maggie closed the door behind Jake. She hadn't seen him since Brian's funeral. With his dark hair and piercing blue eyes, he looked so much like his younger brother that memories of her husband flooded her mind. She sagged against the door, tears slipping down her cheeks.

Back in California, she'd been surrounded by memories of Brian, so many that it hurt to walk around the house they'd shared with their infant son. She'd moved back to Candle Beach and left behind the painful memories, but seeing Jake had brought them all back—the moment she'd watched through the window as the black car pulled up to her on-base house, and then the knock on the door that every military spouse feared. The knock that meant something horrible had happened to her husband.

She shook her head. She'd taken Alex and returned to Candle Beach, intent on starting a new life back home. She'd thrown herself into work at the local diner, eventually purchasing it when the owner retired and making it her own.

Hard work kept the sadness away. She glanced at the wedding picture on an end table. They'd been so young, so happy, when they married. She'd attended college near the university Brian had attended and they'd fallen instantly in love when they met at a local bar. As soon as they both graduated college they'd married and Alex was born five years later.

She paced the hallway, stopping in front of Alex's room.

He slept peacefully, wrapped up in his Spiderman comforter. She smiled and tiptoed back to the main living area.

Should she have invited Jake to stay with them? She looked around the small space. There was room on the couch, but she wasn't sure she wanted anyone to stay at her apartment. He was family, but it felt strange to think of a man sleeping in her home. He'd mentioned staying at a bed and breakfast, so she shouldn't feel too guilty. When she'd talked to her mother-in-law on Thanksgiving, she had said Jake planned to leave for a job with the US Border Patrol soon, so he most likely wouldn't be in town for long.

She'd never thought of Jake as being big on family. According to Brian, his older brother had been quite popular with the ladies but he changed girlfriends often. His relationship preferences were in stark contrast to Brian, who, from the start, had wanted a serious, monogamous relationship and family.

Why was he in Candle Beach anyways? It wasn't exactly somewhere to just pop by on the way to somewhere else. He hadn't visited in the five years that she'd lived there and he hadn't been home to Portland for any of the holidays when she'd visited Brian's family.

He'd caught her off guard tonight, right out of the shower. She blushed, remembering how she'd looked in her ratty old bathrobe. She'd probably resembled a drowned rat with her stringy wet hair. And when he'd pulled her close, she'd pressed against him like a ninny who hadn't been touched by a man in ages—which was actually fairly close to the truth. It had felt good, but he was her brother-in-law, not a date saying goodnight. What-ever. He'd see Alex tomorrow and go back to living his life in the city. Even if she did feel an unexpected physical attraction to him, that was all it was. Nothing would ever come of it.

~

The next day, Jake picked out a blue stuffed whale from a display at Candle Beach Kids and stared at the plush object. What did six-year-olds play with anyways? It had been over thirty years since he was Alex's age. Back then, he and his friends had played race cars on a dirt track, challenging each other to send their cars off the steepest hills they could find. Kids nowadays were more sophisticated though, and he didn't think a Matchbox car would cut it.

"Can I help you find something?" A woman wearing a white Candle Beach Kids T-shirt asked. She smiled and tipped her head at him, causing tendrils of dark hair to escape her bun and prettily frame her face.

"I'm looking for a gift for my nephew. He's six."

"Does he like puzzles? Or drawing? What's he into?"

"I don't know. I think he likes building and creating things." He realized how little he knew about his nephew. His mother had shown him the Lego set she'd bought Alex for Christmas, so he knew Legos were of interest to him. He nestled the whale back into the bin. Shoot, he should have come to visit sooner. He'd promised his brother he'd take care of Maggie and Alex, but he'd let his career get in the way of that promise.

"How about this?" She held up a kid's magnetic science kit. The boy on the front looked to be about eight, with a wondrous smile stretching across his face.

Any kid would love it. He took it from her, turning the box over in his hands to examine it closer. Perfect. "Thanks, I'll take it."

"No problem. Can I help you find anything else?"

"No, this will be all." He placed it on the front counter.

She rang up the science kit. "Are you vacationing in Candle Beach?"

"No, I'm visiting my sister-in-law and nephew. Do you know Maggie Price?"

"Of course, everyone in town knows Maggie." She placed his purchase in a bag emblazoned with the name of the store. "And your nephew must be Alex. He will love the science set." She threw in a small bag of chocolate pirate coins. "On the house."

He smiled gratefully at her. "Thanks, I hope he likes the magnets, but you can never go wrong with candy."

He looked around. Cheerful wicker bins sat on turquoise counters. Shelves lined with T-shirts covered the walls. Tourists would eat it up. "Is this your store?"

"Yes. I'm the owner. Abby." She stuck out her hand and he shook it.

"Nice to meet you. I'm Jake."

"Do you plan to stay in town for long?"

"Not sure. Maybe a week or two. We'll see."

"Well, I know Maggie is really busy, so if you need someone to show you around town, let me know. I grew up here. If you have any questions about Candle Beach, I can probably help." She handed him the bag, allowing her fingers to touch his again. He could tell she was interested in him, but he didn't return the sentiment.

She seemed nice, and normally, she was his type. However, she paled in relation to Maggie. He stopped. What was he talking about? Maggie was his brother's wife. He'd never seen her as a woman before, only as his sister-in-law. So why was he now noticing how she looked and smelled—

and how he felt when she was pressed against his body wearing nothing but a thin bathrobe?

He plucked the bag from Abby's grip. "Thanks. I'll let you know if I need anything else."

She nodded and turned to help another customer, and he rushed out of the shop before any more comparisons or memories came to mind.

5

*J*ake stood outside Maggie's door the next day, feeling like a school kid on his first real date. He held the bag with the magnetic science kit in his right hand and tapped the doorbell with his other hand. The sun shone down on the pavement, creating a feeling of warmth, even if the actual temperature was close to freezing.

Maggie flung the door open. She smiled at him, a genuine gesture that caused his heart to twinge. She wore a casual button-down red-and-black plaid shirt over a pair of slim-fitting blue jeans. Her hair was up and her eyes sparkled. She was as gorgeous as she'd been on her wedding day, seemingly without trying. The scent of roses hung in the air, something he'd now forever associate with her.

"Come in, it's freezing out there." She gestured for him to enter the living room.

He looked around. The walls were painted a welcoming peach color that added depth and cheeriness to the small room. A canvas photograph of Alex as a toddler on the beach held a place of honor behind the couch. Through a cut-through in the wall, he could see the galley kitchen and window where he'd seen Maggie standing the night before.

"Alex!" Maggie called down the hall. "Uncle Jake's here."

The sound of a little boy jumping off a bed and thundering down the hall echoed throughout the small apartment. Alex burst into the room and stopped short in front of him.

"Hi." Alex looked at him with a curious expression. "You don't look like your picture."

"My picture?" Jake asked. When had Alex seen a picture of him?

"Yeah, in Grandma and Grandpa's house. The one on the wall. You're wearing a uniform, like in the picture of my dad."

Right. His commissioning photo. That thing was fifteen years old, no wonder he didn't look the same to Alex. He rubbed the stubble on his chin. And he'd probably been much more clean-shaven then as well.

"That was from a while ago, when I was younger." He held out the bag to Alex. "I brought you this. I wasn't sure what you liked, but this seemed fun."

Alex took the bag from him. Jake shifted his weight and stared at the boy as he opened it. The joy on his face when he saw the gift was the same look Brian used to have as he unwrapped his Christmas presents. In fact, Alex was the spitting image of his little brother. A tear appeared in Jake's eye and he turned sideways to swipe at it.

"Are you okay?" Maggie asked.

"Yeah, I think I got something in my eye." He smiled at her.

"Can we play with it now?" Alex asked as he tore into the box.

Jake checked Maggie's reaction. She nodded.

"Sure, let's set it up on the coffee table." He and Alex removed all the pieces and together, they read through the instructions.

~

Maggie watched her son and his uncle as they hunched over the instruction manual for the gift Jake had brought. Their heads touched, the strands of their dark-brown hair blending imperceptibly. They pressed two of the magnets together and Alex tugged at his piece to break the seal. It broke apart suddenly and he tumbled backwards, laughing the whole time.

"You okay?" Jake asked.

"Do it again!" Alex pressed his magnet to the one his uncle held. Jake acquiesced. Alex repeated the process of pulling the magnet away.

"Now it's Mommy's turn." Alex bounded up from the floor and shoved the magnet at Maggie. She looked at it as if it were a foreign object.

"You just press it to the one he has." Alex pointed to Jake.

Maggie knelt on the floor to reach Jake's outstretched arm. The force of the magnet pulled her closer and their eyes met. The strength of their joined gaze felt as forceful as the magnets they held together. She got goose bumps.

This was exactly how she'd felt the day she met Brian. They'd been sitting next to each other at a bar. She'd turned around on her barstool to get her drink and their eyes had met. Her skin had immediately erupted in goose bumps, and they'd spent every day following that together.

She closed her eyes and then opened them rapidly to

break the spell. It must be something about the Price men. She dropped her hold on the magnet and pushed herself off the ground.

"Uh, I've got to get some things done in the kitchen, okay?" She hurried to the safety of the adjoining kitchen. In the other room, Jake and Alex's voices blended as they continued to try out differing strengths of magnets.

What was that all about? After all these years, was she now attracted to Jake? Or had it simply been too long since she'd been in close contact with a man? She busied herself washing dishes until the ringing of her cell phone interrupted.

"Hello?"

"Hey, Maggie, it's Bernadette. I'm really sorry to bother you, but we had some customers in here that complained about their service and now they want to talk to a manager."

"Where's Elvin?" Maggie said, referring to the assistant manager.

"He had to go to a doctor's appointment."

"Oh, right." She'd completely forgotten she'd approved him leaving his shift for a few hours. "Who are they complaining about?"

"Velma."

She groaned. Of course it was Velma. She needed to get to the café and sort out this mess, but what about Alex? She could leave him with Jake, but they'd only met an hour ago. Was that fair to Jake? He was Alex's uncle though, and he had come to visit him. It was worth asking. She popped back into the room.

"Jake?"

He looked up from the project he was working on with her son. "What's up?"

"I know it's a big imposition, but something came up at work that I really need to take care of. Would you mind staying here with Alex? I should only be gone less than an hour."

"Sure, no problem. Alex and I are getting along fine, right, Alex?"

Her son nodded. "Yeah, Mom, this is so cool."

~

One problem after another hit her at the café. She talked to the couple angered by Velma's lack of service and comped their meal. Then there was a mix-up with the dinner menu. By the time she'd put out all the fires, it was two hours later. She quickly texted Jake to let him know she was on her way home and jumped in the car.

When she got home, Jake and Alex were engaged in a driving video game, Alex giggling as he swerved around the track. "I'm going to beat you this time, Uncle Jake."

"Not unless I let you." Jake made an exaggerated turning movement and uttered a loud car noise, causing Alex to giggle some more.

Maggie hung back in the entry. With the volume up, they hadn't noticed her come in. She hadn't seen her son this happy in a long time. He spent time with his grandfathers, but other than that, there weren't many male role models in his life. Should she have put herself out there in the dating world earlier? She wasn't sure she was ready for that, but maybe she needed to start thinking of Alex's needs too. Then again, the idea of introducing him to someone who might not stick around didn't seem great either.

"Ahem." She cleared her throat. Jake turned around, but Alex kept playing.

"Hey, I didn't hear you come in."

"I know. You guys were too into being speedsters." She laughed. "Sorry it took me so long at work. I really appreciate you staying with Alex. I'm going to make spaghetti and meatballs for dinner. Do you want to stay for dinner, or do you have other plans?"

He grinned. "Nope, no other plans. I'd love to stay. Beats grabbing a sub sandwich from the gas station."

She wrinkled her nose. "Yuck. Next time you think of doing that, stop in at the Bluebonnet Café instead. I may be biased, but our food is pretty darn good."

"Actually, I plan to eat dinner there tomorrow. The owner of the B&B I'm staying at raved about the Thursday meatloaf meal. Perhaps you and Alex would like to join me?"

She mentally checked her work schedule. "That could work. I'm off at six tomorrow. I could have my mom drop Alex off at the café then." She hesitated. "How long are you planning on staying in town? I thought you were starting a new job soon? That's what your mom said."

"I had a positive second interview, but they haven't called back yet. They said it would be another week or two. I'll probably stay in Candle Beach until they do." He smiled easily at her. "Is that okay with you?"

Her stomach lurched as though she'd driven too fast over a hill. Did she want him to stay in town longer? When she thought he was only in town for a day or two, she'd been happy to let him spend time with Alex. Now that he was going to be around for a couple of weeks, Alex would get used to being around Jake and then he'd suddenly be out of his life like he'd been since Brian died. And what about the way she felt around Jake? She wasn't sure she was comfortable with those feelings.

"Mom? Is Uncle Jake going to come visit again?" Alex peered at her hopefully.

She couldn't take away time with his uncle for fear of what Jake leaving would do to him. She met Jake's gaze and forced a smile. "Yep, he's going to be around for a couple of weeks. Isn't that great?"

6

_F_riday rolled around and Jake was still in town. Alex had seen him every day since Tuesday and the two of them had become fast friends. When Maggie left for work, they were busy building a giant city out of Legos.

Work was exhausting and she'd scheduled a cake-tasting appointment at the café with Dahlia right after she finished her shift. She'd offered to make Dahlia and Garrett's wedding cake as a gift, but now she wondered if that had been such a good idea.

"Which do you like better, the carrot cake, chocolate fudge, or vanilla bean cake?" Maggie eyed her friends and held her pen over her notepad. The engaged couple had been deliberating over their choice of cakes for an hour already.

"Chocolate," Dahlia said, at the same time as Garrett said, "Vanilla."

They laughed in unison and Maggie shook her head. She smiled at them. "Opposites attract, huh?"

Dahlia laughed again and hugged his arm. "Can we

intersperse layers of chocolate and vanilla? Maybe with raspberry in between?"

He nodded in agreement and they peered at Maggie hopefully.

She calculated how long it would take her to make the more complicated cake. It would easily double the time she'd allotted to it and she'd planned to make a practice cake first. It had been a while since she used fondant, and if her skills with petit fours were any indication, she'd need all the time she could get to make the wedding cake. Her friends gazed at her expectantly. She couldn't let them down.

She forced a smile on her face. "Sure, I can do that. No problem."

Dahlia beamed and got up to hug her. "Thanks, Maggie. Now, how should we decorate it?"

Maggie sighed inwardly. With Dahlia and Garrett being so different, who knew how long this could take? She looked at her watch. She was supposed to pick up Alex at her parent's house in thirty minutes.

Jake had dropped him off with them in the afternoon because he had an appointment of some sort. He hadn't been specific about it. In fact, he'd been rather secretive. Not that it was any of her business. He probably had a hot date or something. A rush of jealousy came over her and she slammed her pen down on the table in front of her.

Dahlia raised an eyebrow and Maggie smiled weakly. "Sorry, I just realized I forgot one of my decorating books at home."

"I'm sure you're full of great ideas," Garrett said pleasantly.

She relaxed. This was supposed to be a fun project and a wedding gift for one of her best friends. "You know, I was thinking about purple flowers on the top of the white fondant and then a simple beading along the edges." She flipped the cake look book open to show them the style she recommended.

"I love it," Dahlia squealed.

"Me too." Garrett put his arm around his bride-to-be and kissed her squarely on the mouth. "Our wedding will be perfect, with the most beautiful bride ever."

Maggie's stomach twisted. They were so lucky to have found each other. When they'd first met, they hadn't thought so, but after a few months, they'd realized their differences were what made them perfect for each other.

Brian had been a lot like Maggie—a Type A personality, driven to succeed. While his brother Jake had taken a more circuitous journey through the military ranks, Brian had completed ROTC in college and been commissioned as Second Lieutenant immediately following graduation. He'd intended to stay in the military and retire as a General.

A tear slipped from Maggie's eye. She'd been thinking about Brian a lot lately and she blamed Jake for that. Before he showed up in Candle Beach, she'd done her best to put any thoughts of her deceased husband out of her mind. Seeing Jake every day had brought back so many memories.

"Maggie?" Dahlia asked.

She'd been staring into space for who knew how long. Her friends both had their eyes on her.

"Sorry guys, I was imagining how the cake would look," she lied.

"Are you sure this won't be too much for you?" Dahlia asked. "You know I'd love for you to make the cake, but if it's too much with the catering and all, I can have someone in Haven Shores make it."

Maggie waved her hand. "Don't worry about it. I want to

make your cake. I have staff at the restaurant to help with the catering." That was partially true, but her staff was reduced for the winter and with the holiday tourists, the café would be near full capacity. Now, with Bernadette leaving in a week, things would be even shorter staffed in the kitchen. The entire café staff would be stretched thin. She wrote down Dahlia and Garrett's decoration and cake layer choices in her notebook.

"Okay, we're done with the cake choices. Can you get me your final count for the dinner reception by next Wednesday?"

"Definitely." Garrett stood and shook her hand.

"Thanks, Maggie. I'm so glad I have you to help with this. We'd probably be having hot dogs on the beach if it weren't for you." Dahlia wrapped her arm around Maggie's shoulder.

Garrett made a face at his fiancée. "Yes, thank goodness for Maggie. I hate hot dogs." Dahlia swatted him and he grabbed her hand to pull her close, kissing her again.

"Dinner?" he asked. Dahlia nodded and waved goodbye to Maggie.

Maggie waved back and watched her friends as they exited her office hand in hand. Maybe someday, when Alex was older, she'd find the same happiness that they shared.

~

"Mom, can we invite Uncle Jake over for family movie night?" Alex asked as he ran out to the car. The sky was getting dark earlier as the days grew closer to the winter solstice. Maggie stared out at the shadowy night. It was only December and she'd already had enough of winter. The summer sunshine couldn't come fast enough to suit her.

She weighed her options, jangling her car keys. They'd seen Jake every day since he'd arrived. She had to admit, he'd turned out to be a better uncle than she'd have guessed. He seemed attentive to Alex and interested in what he had to say. And it was actually kind of nice to have another adult around at home. She hadn't realized how thirsty she was for adult companionship. Her best friends were involved with their significant others and didn't have as much time for her as they used to.

"Sure, honey, we can invite him. But he had something going on today, so I don't know if he'll be able to make it." Jake's secretive afternoon appointment niggled at her. Why wouldn't he tell her where he was going?

She texted him and asked him to come over for dinner and a movie. It was almost like she was asking him for a date. If you considered having a six-year-old sitting in between you during the movie as a date. She laughed at the thought. Of course it wasn't a date. That was silly.

Alex gave her a funny look. "What's so funny?"

"Nothing." She smiled reassuringly at him. "I was thinking about the movie we rented." Her phone beeped to alert her to an incoming text message.

Sounds good. Almost done here, see you in thirty minutes.

Her heart raced and she wasn't sure why. Probably just the prospect of having another adult around on a Friday night, something she hadn't experienced in a while. The sense of anticipation persisted until Jake arrived thirty minutes later.

After the pizza delivery driver arrived with their pepperoni pizza, they sat down to watch a Pixar movie she'd rented from the grocery store. Many of the jokes and innu-endos embedded in the movie were over Alex's head, but she and Jake caught them and exchanged amused glances.

He'd stopped at the grocery store for a bottle of wine and salad mix, so while her son drank his root beer, they enjoyed glasses of red wine. She rested her head against the back of the couch, enjoying the flavor of the wine and relaxing. This was nice. She and Brian used to do at-home movie dates when he'd been a broke Second Lieutenant, and it remained as one of her fondest memories of their relationship.

The credits rolled and Alex jumped up from the couch.

"Can we play a game? Please, Mom, please?"

She looked at the clock. It was only a little past seven on a Friday night. "Sure, we can play a quick game, but bedtime at eight, okay?" She turned to Jake. "Do you want to stay for a board game? Alex is a big fan of Trouble."

"I'm a Trouble master. Are you sure you want to take me on?" Jake asked his nephew. He wiggled his eyebrows and Alex giggled.

"Yeah, I'm going to win." Alex beamed and ran over to the closet where they kept the games. He stood on his tiptoes, trying in vain to get to the board game.

"Let me help you with that." Jake reached over him and pulled the game down, handing it to him. He turned and ruffled Alex's hair as her son scooted past him. His gaze was thoughtful and he regarded Alex with more tenderness than she'd expect. Was this really the same guy who Brian had sworn would never settle down? Maybe her mother-in-law would get grandkids from Jake after all. He'd make a good father and it would be nice for Alex to have some cousins.

They settled down on the floor around the coffee table. True to his word, Jake was excellent at Trouble. When he trounced them, she expected Alex to throw a tantrum. He wasn't known as a happy loser.

Instead, he asked, "Can we do this again tomorrow?"

Jake looked at her with raised eyebrows and said, "That's up to your mom."

"Sorry, honey, you're staying with Grandma and Grandpa tomorrow night. I've got to work late." She placed the game board into the box. Jake put the cover on it and returned it to the game closet.

"Oh." Alex was visibly disappointed. "But I want to see Uncle Jake."

"I think he'll be here for a few more days, right, Jake?" He nodded. She clapped her hands. "Now, time for bed for little boys."

Alex scampered off down the hallway then called from the bathroom, "Can Uncle Jake tuck me in and read me a bedtime story?"

The pizza churned in her stomach. She always read him a story as part of their nightly ritual. She looked at Jake, who shrugged. "Yes, get your teeth brushed and he'll be there in a minute." Her words felt hollow. It was weird to have someone else in her house sharing the bedtime duties.

Jake read to Alex from the chapter book that he and Maggie read from every night. She stood in the hallway where they couldn't see her and peeked into his room. Alex listened raptly and when they were done, Jake kissed him on the cheek. A huge smile spread across her son's face. She backed away before either of them caught her spying and busied herself tidying up in the kitchen.

"I didn't mean to step on your nightly routine," Jake said in his deep voice as he came up behind her.

She glanced at him before placing a cup in the dishwasher. "It's fine. I'm glad for him to have more family around and I know you won't be able to stay in town much longer, so it's good for him to spend time with you while he can."

It did worry her that Alex seemed to be growing more and more attached to his uncle. It would kill him when Jake had to leave Candle Beach.

"Do you plan to come back to visit?" she asked in what she hoped was a light tone. "Alex would love to see you."

"And you? Would you like me to come back?"

She felt him watching her. "Of course. It's been nice spending time with some of Brian's family. Your parents aren't able to come visit very often and Alex sees my family all the time."

"Well, I hope to spend a lot more time in Candle Beach, so I'm glad to hear that."

"You should come back in summer. It's beautiful here then and not so gray."

"I'll take that into consideration." He smiled at her. "Well, it's getting late, I should be going." He paused, as if waiting for her to object.

She wanted to ask him to stay, if only for a little longer, but she couldn't make the words come out of her mouth. He put his jacket on and left. Her stomach twisted as she watched his car disappear around a corner. Spending time with Jake had been nice, but for her sake and Alex's, she couldn't let him get too close.

7

"So you were Military Police with the Army for the last twenty years?" Candle Beach's Police Chief Aaron Lee ran his finger over Jake's resume, then leaned back in his chair and peered into Jake's eyes. Above his head, framed degrees and commendations hung on the wall. File cabinets lined the other sides of the room. Every available space was covered with paper, but Jake suspected Chief Lee knew the exact location of every document he needed.

"Yes, sir. I retired as a Major. I was an enlisted soldier and then after a few years, commissioned into the Army through their Green to Gold program." Jake put his arms on the desk and pointed at the education section of his resume. "I attained my degree in Criminal Justice while in the service."

"Well, this opening is for an entry-level role. Is that something you're interested in?"

"Yes. I know my prior experience and education would make me a good fit for the position. I realize I'm a little older than your typical applicant, but I think I'm probably a little wiser as well."

Chief Lee chuckled and shook his head. "You should see some of the kids I get in here applying for a job with the Candle Beach police force. They think they know everything."

"I know the type—I used to be one of them back in the day." Jake grinned. "But in all seriousness, I want to stay in Candle Beach."

"Right." Jake could feel Chief Lee's eyes on him. "You're from the city. Why would you want to work for a police force in the middle of nowhere? I mean, we love our small town and everything, but it isn't for everyone."

"I understand your concern. But I have family here, and after spending half of my life devoted to the Army, I want to settle down and spend time with them. This town is great. I've met so many new people in the small amount of time I've been here, and everyone is so friendly." With a start, he realized how much he wanted to stay in town. He'd gone back down to Portland for his Border Patrol interview the Tuesday after he first arrived in Candle Beach and then turned right back around the next day for his second interview with the Candle Beach Police Department. Driving down Main Street that morning had been like coming home.

The police chief smiled at him. "That's how I ended up here. I used to work in the city, but I came to the beach for a vacation with my family, and the wife and I never wanted to leave." He pushed his chair away from the desk and stood, then walked over to Jake and extended his hand. Jake rose and shook it firmly.

"After our Human Resources Manager met with you on Friday afternoon, she highly recommended you for the position," the Chief continued. "But the final decision is mine, and you've given me a lot to think about. I'll be in touch." He held the door open for Jake. The sugary smell of donuts wafted through the room.

"Thank you, sir. I appreciate it."

Jake left the interview with a bounce in his step. Was he really doing this? Thinking about staying in Candle Beach? A job with a small-town police department would be very different than working for the Border Patrol—if the federal government even called him back about the position he'd interviewed for. Candle Beach had its own allure though. Alex was here and he'd grown attached to him in the short time they'd spent together. And then there was Maggie. He'd promised his brother that he'd look after them, and now that he was free to make his own career decisions he planned to make good on that promise.

～

Maggie had to laugh at her son's antics. He hadn't stopped moving since she'd told him Jake would be there in ten minutes.

"When is he coming over?" Alex bounced on his toes on their thick living room carpet. "I want to show him how good I'm getting at Mario Kart."

"He'll be here soon." Alex had insisted on having Jake over for dinner. He'd gone back to Portland for a few days, but had come back to stay in Candle Beach for the next week. She wondered again if she should have invited him to stay at their apartment instead of in a B&B. Probably better to not let him get closer though. It would be hard enough for Alex when his uncle moved up north for his new job with the Border Patrol.

An image of Jake sitting on the couch, laughing at a joke in the movie, came to mind. She'd miss him too, although the more time she spent with him, the stronger the physical attraction became. His easy banter had turned to flirting and it seemed like he felt it too. With him leaving though, there was no way she was going to act on anything. Given their family dynamics, that was probably for the best.

Someone knocked on the door and Alex ran to it, flinging it open.

"Alex!" Maggie admonished him. "You can't just open the door without finding out who it is first."

"But it's Uncle Jake. I knew it would be," he said, certain of his choice in his six-year-old logic.

She sighed. "Right, but you didn't know it was him for sure."

"But it was." He dismissed her concerns and wrapped his arms around his uncle's waist.

Maggie gave up and looked at the new arrival. She sucked in her breath. Jake hadn't been around for a few days and if anything, his spell on her was even stronger. He wore a tight-fitting knit shirt that hugged his biceps and she had a hard time taking her eyes off him. He carried a yellow bag from the Lego store, a bottle of wine and a small bouquet of flowers.

"Hey, Alex. This is for you. I went shopping while I was in Portland and I thought you'd like it." Jake gently disentangled his nephew from his waist so he could walk through the door, and handed him the Lego bag.

"Hey, Maggie. These are for you." He held out the flowers and his eyes met hers. "I wanted to thank you for welcoming me into your home over the past week." His easy smile seemed to reach inside her and melt her heart. She took the flowers from him and sniffed a red rose in the mixed bouquet. She loved roses, but didn't usually buy them for herself because of the expense.

"Uh, thank you. They're beautiful." She turned and called over her shoulder, "I'm going to put these in some water." Alone in the kitchen she sat down on the floor in front of the sink to reach into the cabinet where she kept vases. What was happening? Was the attraction due to his resemblance to Brian? Or maybe because she was finally opening herself up to dating again? Whatever it was, nothing could happen between them.

The oven timer beeped, so she grabbed the first vase she found and stuffed the flowers in it. At the sink, she filled the vase with water and set it on the counter before pulling a steaming pan of lasagna out of the oven and tossing the salad.

"Food's ready, guys."

They piled into the kitchen, Alex talking a mile a minute about the new Lego set his uncle had bought him. Jake devoured the pasta dish and complimented her on her cooking. It was nice to have someone to cook for, as her son was often a picky eater.

After Alex was in bed, they sat around the kitchen table drinking the wine that Jake had brought.

"So, I have some news." He set his wine glass down on the Formica-topped vintage table she'd found at a swap meet.

"What?" Her heart beat faster. Was this it? Had the Border Patrol called him for the job? She knew he'd be leaving soon, but had hoped for Alex's sake that he could stay a bit longer. "Are you leaving Candle Beach?"

"No. Actually, that's what I wanted to talk with you about." He scanned her face. "How would you feel about me staying in town?"

"You mean for another couple of weeks? Or what?"

"Chief Lee offered me a position with the Candle Beach Police Department. The town is growing and they had an entry-level opening."

"Wait, what?" Maggie gulped from her wine glass. What was he talking about? He'd never mentioned any interest in being a policeman. Was this what his secretive meeting on Friday had been about?

"Well, you know I was an MP in the Army. I have a degree in Criminal Justice and this seemed like a perfect fit. After spending time with you and Alex, I've realized I want to be with family, not up north working at the border."

She stared at him and poured another glass of wine.

"So what do you think?" he asked.

"I think it seems very sudden," she said honestly. He'd only been in town for a little over a week and now he was making a huge decision based on her and her son.

"I've spent my whole life doing what the Army wanted me to do. This is something I feel certain about. I'll start out as a rookie and they're sending me to training near Seattle in January. Until then, I'll mainly be working the desk and learning the ropes."

"Wow. So you're moving here." She gulped down more wine. "That's great."

"You don't seem too happy about it." He placed his hand on her arm. Her skin burned pleasantly where his fingers touched her, sending an electric shock throughout her body. She moved her arm off the table, away from his touch, and brushed her hair back.

"Of course I'm happy. Alex will love having you here. I'm just surprised. You never seemed like the type of person who would be happy in a small town."

He looked at her. "Maybe you don't know me as well as you think you do."

She met his gaze and her pulse quickened. "Maybe you're right."

"I'd like to be a part of Alex's life." He sighed. "I miss my brother. I wish he could have seen what a wonderful kid he had."

Maggie's eyes turned unbidden to their wedding portrait on the end table near the kitchen and tears welled in her eyes. "I miss him too." She got up and placed her wine glass carefully in the sink. "I've got to turn in soon. I have an early shift at the café tomorrow."

He followed suit. "I should get home too. I promised Chief Lee I'd be there at eight o'clock sharp tomorrow morning."

She walked him to the door. "Congratulations on the new job." She gave him a quick hug, determined not to let those pesky feelings of attraction stop her from how she'd normally react to good news.

He smiled at her. "Thanks. I'll see you soon."

She watched him go, unsure of how she was feeling. Now that he was staying in Candle Beach, should she say something to him about her growing attraction to him? Or was that a recipe for disaster? She didn't want to jeopardize Alex's relationship with his uncle. It was too important. With Dahlia's wedding and Christmas right around the corner, she had enough on her plate. No need to add relationship drama to the mix.

8

*M*aggie leaned forward in her desk chair with her hands threaded through her hair at the temples and her elbows resting on the wooden desk surface. She eyed the closed door to her office and allowed herself to scream silently. *Aaahh.* She was about ready to tear her hair out. It was a little over a week until Dahlia's wedding and her friend kept changing the final attendee count. She'd expected there to be some issues when catering a wedding, but not this many. She took a deep breath and shuffled through the wedding reception paperwork until she found the menu that Garrett and Dahlia had decided on.

With the current food order, she'd need to rework some of the entrees and make the buffet portions slightly smaller to accommodate the last-minute changes. There was a slight chance that her supplier might be able to get her extra food on short notice so she wouldn't have to decrease the portion sizes. She fired off an e-mail to the supplier and crossed her fingers.

Her cell phone lit up and vibrated across the desk.

"Hello?" she asked without viewing the caller.

"Hi, honey!"

Her mother sounded more excited than Maggie had heard her in years. "What's up?" She used a pen to circle some of the dinner selections on the menu, only half listening to her mother's babbles.

"So we leave tomorrow for our big adventure," she said gleefully.

She had Maggie's full attention now.

"I'm sorry, did you say you were going somewhere? Tomorrow?" She usually babysat Alex when Maggie worked nights. Where would she find another babysitter on such short notice?

"Yes. We're finally taking a cruise. Mary Ellen Schultz, you know, my friend from church? Well, she found a fantastic last-minute deal on a cruise to the Caribbean and your dad and I are going to join them. We fly out to Florida tomorrow and the ship leaves on Saturday."

Maggie pulled the phone away from her face and stared at it for a moment before pressing it back to her ear.

"Oh, but don't worry. I worked it out with the neighbor's girl. She's on winter break from college already and she's happy to babysit Alex when you need her. I know this is kind of last minute, so we'll cover the cost of hiring her."

Maggie didn't know what to say. Her parents were incredibly generous to help so much with Alex and they did need a vacation. They hadn't been anywhere in years, and a Caribbean vacation sounded amazing. But what did they know about this girl from next door? She hadn't left Alex alone with a stranger before.

"Have you known the babysitter for long? I'm just not sure about leaving Alex with someone I've never met." She chewed on the end of her pen.

"I've known Stacey and her family for years. She used to

babysit all the little kids in the neighborhood before she went away to college. Do you want to come over and meet her tonight?"

She checked her schedule. She could fit in a meeting when she picked up Alex from her parents' house that night. "Sure, I can interview her when I get Alex from you. Can you check if that's okay with her?"

"Of course. Honey, you know we wouldn't leave Alex with just anyone. Stacey's a good girl." Her mother squealed. "And we're so excited about this trip. Can you imagine getting out of this dreary weather and sunbathing in December? I can't wait."

"It sounds lovely." She gazed out the window. The skies were gray and rain drizzled onto the pavement in the café's back parking lot. "I'd love to go somewhere warm."

"Your father even said he'd buy a new bathing suit. He hasn't bought any new clothes in a decade."

Maggie smiled. Her father was a cheapskate and always insisted his clothes were fine. He must be really excited if he was buying something new. "I hope you have a wonderful time. Do you need me to feed your cats or anything?"

"Yes, I was hoping you could take care of them and bring in the mail. Maybe you could come in the morning and evening to feed them?"

"I can do that. I'll make sure everything is good at your house. Just have fun." An e-mail popped up on her screen. "Mom, I've got to go. I'll see you in a few hours, okay?"

"See you later," her mother sang out.

Some of her mother's excitement carried over to Maggie and she felt her lips spread into a joyful smile. It was good to hear her mother so happy. She clicked on the new e-mail. Yes! Her supplier said the changes were no problem. Now she wouldn't have to cut the portion sizes or disappoint her friend. She opened her office door to the kitchen and listened for a moment. The normal sounds of her staff cooking for the lunch rush were the only thing she heard. The smell of meatloaf wafted into the small space, making her stomach rumble. Everything seemed to be running smoothly today at the café. Things were looking up.

Her phone rang again—probably her mother with more cruise details. With a smile on her face, she picked up the phone and answered it.

"Hello?"

"Hi, Mrs. Price. This is Sue from the office at Bluebonnet Lake Elementary."

Maggie's heart dropped to her knees. Why was someone from Alex's school calling her?

"Is Alex okay? What happened?"

"Oh, I'm sorry to have worried you. Alex is fine." Sue paused. "I'm actually calling because he has been having some behavioral issues on the playground. He's been rather aggressive with some of his friends. Today, I had to separate him from some of the other boys because he tackled them during what was supposed to be a friendly flag football game."

"Oh." Her mind raced. What was going on with him?

"You don't need to come and pick him up today, but if this behavior continues, we may need to discuss a behavioral discipline plan."

"Of course," Maggie said automatically. "And I'll be sure to discuss it with him this evening."

"I'm sure it will all work out fine. Please let us know if you have any questions or if we can be of help."

"Thank you." She hung up the phone. Her feeling of elation over the supplier's e-mail had been replaced with dread. She managed to hang on for the rest of her shift, but couldn't help worrying about Alex for the rest of the day.

That evening, she let herself into her parents' house and almost tripped over three suitcases lined up by the door. Her mother met her in the entrance hall and she relayed what the school had told her.

"He's getting into trouble at school?" Her mom looked puzzled. "That doesn't sound like Alex."

"Yeah, I don't know what's going on. I'm going to talk with him when we get home."

"Well, good luck." Alex ran past her, out the door, and her mom raised her eyebrows and shrugged. "He was fine earlier."

When they got home, Maggie asked Alex to sit down on the couch. "So I got a call from school today." She eyed her son.

Alex squirmed on his seat cushion and played with his shirt to avoid looking at her.

"Do you want to tell me why you tackled your friend?" Maggie searched his face.

He sighed. "Max teased me about not having a dad, so I pushed him. I didn't want to tell Ms. Sue the real reason, so I said it was because we were playing touch football and I got too rough." A tear slipped out the corner of his eye.

Maggie moved to sit next to Alex and wrapped her arm around him. "Sweetie, I'm so sorry that boy teased you. That wasn't right of him to do that. You know, you do have a dad, and he'd have given anything to be here with you right now. He loved you so much." She kissed the top of his head. "But next time someone says something like that, either walk away or tell the teacher instead of pushing him, okay?"

He nodded and she sent him off to get ready for bed. When he had brushed his teeth and put his pajamas on, she read a chapter with him of the novel they were reading and kissed him on the forehead. "Goodnight, sweetie."

He closed his eyes. She waited outside his door until she heard him softly snoring.

Alex had never complained too much about not having a dad, but she'd known it would come up at some point. Now she had to figure out how to make things better for him. He needed a man in his life. Having Jake around was a good start, but she still didn't think she could count on him to stick around.

~

The next day, things seemed better with Alex. Of course, he'd only been at school for part of a day since then, but still —there hadn't been any more phone calls from the administrative staff. Chalk that up in the win column. Her parents had left already to catch a plane from Seattle to Miami to board their cruise on Saturday, so this would be the first evening that Alex spent with a babysitter.

She'd met Stacey, and had actually liked her. Things were going her way.

That was, until Stacey called to say she'd caught the flu and wouldn't be able to babysit that night.

"I'm really sorry, Mrs. Price." She coughed. "I've never been this sick in my life. It hit me like a freight train this morning. I must have caught something on the airplane coming home from college."

What was she supposed to say to that? Stacey obviously felt bad. "It's okay, I'll figure something out. I hope you feel better. Get some rest."

School would be dismissed in a few hours and she was out a babysitter. She didn't want to bother Jake. He'd started his new job the day before and probably had a lot going on. She called everyone she could think of first and then reluctantly dialed her brother-in-law when she ran out of other options.

~

"Tonight?" Jake asked. Maggie had called him at the last minute to ask if he could babysit that night. Not that he minded.

"Yeah, the babysitter canceled. She's sick and my parents are out of town. Can you do it?" Maggie sighed through the phone. "I know you just started your new job, and I wouldn't ask otherwise, but I'm out of options."

He wasn't sure whether to be happy that she'd thought to ask him, or offended that he was her last resort.

"I worked a morning shift today, so I'm actually home now. I'd love to see Alex. He owes me a rematch of Mario Kart."

"Great." The relief in her voice was evident. "He's done with school at three thirty. Do you know how to get to his school?"

"I do. I'll be there to pick him up." He set his phone back on the nightstand and looked around. Maggie was finally accepting him in Alex's life and he was settling down in Candle Beach. His little room at the B&B wasn't going to cut it much longer. He wanted somewhere where he could make a meal or play his music without fear of waking up the neighbor. And with his savings and the low housing costs in Candle Beach, he should be able to afford something decent. That was something Candle Beach had over living in the big city. There may not be much nightlife, but at least he could afford a home.

He still hadn't heard anything from the government about the Border Patrol job, but it didn't really matter. At this point, he was committed to staying in town and he looked forward to getting involved in small-town life.

~

Alex was ecstatic to see Jake when he picked him up from school. He jumped up and down and tugged at Jake's arm.

"Uncle Jake, can I introduce you to my friends?" He yanked on Jake's hand, not giving him an option to say no. He allowed his nephew to pull him over to where a group of young boys stood. Their moms were grouped next to them, chattering away to each other.

"This is my Uncle Jake," Alex said proudly to his friends. "He was in the Army and went to Iraq."

The boys stared at him like Alex had told them that his uncle had invented the Nerf gun.

"Whoa," a tall, towheaded boy said. "Did you shoot anyone?"

Jake smiled. Kids always asked him that question. "Well..."

The curious kid's mother overheard and approached Jake. "I'm sorry, sir, he's pretty blunt. You don't have to answer him." She cocked her head to the side. "I haven't seen you around before. Are you a relative of Alex's?"

"I'm his uncle. I just moved to town after getting out of the Army."

She appraised him from head to toe and gave him a thousand-watt smile. "Well, thank you for your service. If you need someone to show you around town, let me know."

He smiled at her and took Alex's hand. He never knew what to say when people thanked him for his military service. While he was proud of what he'd done, it seemed strange to be thanked by a stranger for doing your job.

After they were half a block away from the elementary school, Alex turned to Jake and said, "That was so cool. Max is always bragging about his dad being a scientist, but being in the Army is even better."

"Your dad was in the Army too, you know."

"Yeah, I know." Alex frowned. "But I never really got to know him. He died when I was a baby. I wish he was here so Max wouldn't make fun of me for not having a dad."

Jake's throat tightened. Did Maggie know how much Alex missed having a father present in his life?

He stopped and knelt on the ground in front of Alex. He looked his nephew straight in the eye. "Your dad would have loved you so much. Correction, he did love you. He used to call me and tell me all the cute things you did as a baby." The boy's face had crumpled and tears streamed down his cheeks. Jake hugged him. "If you ever need me, I'll be there for you."

Alex turned his face up, a glimmer of hope stretching across his face. "You promise?"

"Promise."

"Hey," Alex whispered. "Do you want to see my friends and my secret hiding place?"

"Uh, sure." What kind of hiding place could a little kid possibly have?

Alex led him to a dilapidated white house a few blocks away. The windows were boarded up on the main floor, and the upstairs windows had been broken. A chain-link fence surrounded the property. It probably looked like an interesting place to a little kid, but to him it just looked dangerous.

"I don't think you're supposed to play here, buddy."

"All my friends do. Don't tell Mom though. She'd get upset." He rested his backpack against the fence and pulled at a broken section to allow entrance to the backyard. "See? It's easy to get in here."

Jake stared at the kid's backpack, its bright colors a stark contrast to the run-down house's dirty, flaking exterior.

He got down to Alex's level. "I don't want you playing here anymore." He pointed to the sagging porch steps. "Do you see those steps over there? Anyone walking on them could go through the wood at any time. This place is rotting and needs to be torn down." He looked Alex directly in the eye.

"Yes, sir," Alex mumbled, his face crestfallen. "We don't come here very often anyways."

"Good. I'm just getting to know you and I don't want anything bad to happen to you, okay?"

"Okay."

Jake grabbed his hand and led him down the street to Maggie's apartment. He used the key she'd left under the mat to unlock the door. When she got home, he needed to give her a lecture about safety. This may be a small town, but two days at the police department had taught him that even Candle Beach sometimes had problems.

He helped Alex with a short math assignment and then they turned on Mario Kart.

Alex screwed up his face in concentration as he veered from side to side in sync with his race car. "I'm winning, I'm winning," he shrieked.

Jake had to hide his smile. He'd been playing with only one hand as a handicap.

Alex's car soared across the finish line.

"Good job! I guess you are the master of Mario Kart." He

put down his controller and gave Alex a high five, and a smile stretched across his nephew's face.

Then Jake stood and stretched. "I'm going to the kitchen for something to drink. Do you want anything? A glass of milk?"

"No, thanks." Alex was captivated by the highlights reel of their recent race.

Jake filled a glass with ice water from the fridge and leaned against the doorway to the kitchen. The little boy looked so much like Brian had as a child. He thought again about how much Brian would have loved seeing his son grow up. Any man would be proud to have a kid as special as Alex. Or, for that matter, to be married to Maggie. His brother had been lucky to have them in his life, if only for such a short time.

He himself had felt such joy being in their lives since he arrived in town. From the moment he'd seen Maggie again, he'd known he was physically attracted to her, and that attraction had grown to include mental and emotional components as well. He'd never felt this way before. Maggie seemed reluctant to consider him as anything other than Brian's older brother, but he thought she may be warming to him.

His eyes caught on Maggie and Brian's wedding photo on the end table by the kitchen. Both his brother and Maggie wore huge smiles as they stared into each other's eyes, consumed by their love for each other.

What would Brian think if he were to ask Maggie out on a date? Would he be upset? He glanced back to Alex. His brother had asked him to help with his wife and son, but he probably hadn't intended for them to be romantically involved. Was he moving in on Brian's family? Trying to take what should have been his brother's?

He shook his head. He couldn't think like that. Brian was gone and nothing could bring him back and make his little family whole again. Jake needed to look towards the future, and what he saw there was a chance at happiness for Maggie, Alex, and himself.

9

*S*now had fallen in Candle Beach overnight, just in time for the annual winter festival. Jake knocked on the door to Maggie's apartment and breathed in the crisp, cool air while he waited for her to answer it. Had it really only been a week and a half since he'd arrived in Candle Beach? When he'd arrived, he'd had nothing, and now he had deepening family ties and a job with the police department.

"Hey." Maggie opened the door and smiled at him. She wore a long-sleeved cotton shirt and blue jeans that hugged her curves. "We're almost ready to go. She thrust a thermos of coffee at him. "We'll want this later." She turned backward to yell, "Alex, let's go!" His nephew skipped into the room.

Jake took the coffee from her and leaned against the doorframe, gazing at the empty street outside and enjoying the juxtaposition of warmth from her apartment and the icy coldness of the outdoors.

When she came out, she'd dressed both herself and Alex in fluffy winter jackets. Her apartment was a little too far from the Marina Park to walk in the winter, so she drove them there in her Prius.

When she'd invited him to join her and Alex at the winter festival, he hadn't known what it would be like. It turned out to be a big town event. He recognized several new acquaintances and waved at them.

"This is my favorite time of year." Maggie twirled around in the middle of the Marina Park. Twinkly white lights hung in all the trees and a light dusting of snow coated the ground like powdered sugar. She opened her mouth and stuck out her tongue to catch a stray snowflake. A group of people turned in her direction and smiled before returning to their conversation.

"Mom, stop that." Alex shuffled his feet around in the snow, clearly embarrassed by her antics. He turned to Jake. "Can you make her stop?"

He laughed. "Your mom's happy. Let her be."

Maggie shot him a grateful smile.

"So, what's on the agenda?" Jake reviewed the huge schedule posted on the bulletin board by the gazebo. It listed in blue paint a full day's worth of activities that the Chamber of Commerce had planned.

"I've been coming to the winter festival since I was a kid. It's one of my favorite childhood memories." She pointed to one of the items on the list. "How about sandcastle building at the beach? That's always my favorite thing to do during the festival."

"Sandcastles? In the middle of December?" Jake stared at her dubiously.

"It's winter time on the coast. We don't get much snow accumulation for a snowman-building contest, so we have to use what we do have—sand. They aren't all sandcastles, more like sand sculptures of whatever you want."

"Sounds fun." He picked up a brochure and leafed through it. "Maybe we can check out the pie-eating contest later?" His mouth salivated at the thought of freshly baked pies.

Alex sulked. "I don't want to build a sandcastle."

Maggie gave her son the evil eye and said sternly, "Let's go." She took his hand and pulled him toward the beach overlook.

When they arrived at the overlook, she pointed out the crowd of people a hundred feet from the foot of the stairs. Like them, everyone in the crowd was dressed for winter. Jake found it humorous to see people hanging out on the sand in the dead of winter. Instead of wearing bathing suits to lounge in the sun, they wore puffy jackets and snow or rain boots.

They walked down the icy stairs to the sandcastle-building contest headquarters. Down on the beach, the sand was clear of snow.

"Where's the snow?" Alex craned his head from side to side, searching for white powder.

"When the snow hits the beach, it melts because of all the salt in the sand, just like when we put salt on the side-walk." Maggie took his hand and dragged him over to where a tall man with a clipboard and a portly woman were giving out instructions.

"We'd like to enter the family contest."

"Sure." The man consulted his clipboard and then pointed down the beach. "Do you see where that large family is down there?"

She nodded. A family with at least four kids and two sets of grandparents were hard at work building an immense sand structure.

"You can take the area of beach next to them. Good

luck." He handed her a piece of paper with the contest rules on it.

She beamed at Alex and Jake. "So? Are you guys ready for some fun?"

Jake looked at the beach. Making sand castles on a soggy beach, wearing a parka in the middle of winter, wasn't exactly his idea of fun. But, it was obviously important to Maggie.

He pasted a smile on his face and pumped his fist in the air. "Let's go make a sandcastle!"

Alex glared at him, but he grabbed his nephew's hand and tugged at him until he followed his mother over to their designated building location.

"So what should we build?"

"An igloo?" Jake suggested. It made sense in the freezing weather.

She smiled at him with condescension. "Half of these teams are making igloos. Get creative, Price."

"Fine, fine." He thought for a moment. "How about a Christmas tree? We could build it lying on the ground instead of standing up, but you'd know what it was from above."

She considered his suggestion. "I like it. We'll need ornaments and a nice star though."

Jake eyed Alex. "Your mom takes this very seriously."

"I know. She does this every year." He sighed and looked enviously at a family ascending the beach stairs to town.

Jake shivered, but Maggie didn't appear affected by the chilly weather. She instructed them on how to form the individual tree branches and ornaments so they'd look more realistic. Two hours later, when every part of his body was frozen, he thought it was done, but she stared at it, tapping her chin with her finger.

"It's missing something."

"What?" Most of the other contestants had finished, and while he had to admit that their Christmas tree looked nicer than the neighboring family's igloo, he envied them being off the beach, probably drinking hot cocoa in the town square. He pulled out the thermos of coffee and took a swig of it. It was lukewarm, but tasted fine.

"Presents," Maggie said. "We forgot to make presents for under the tree." She scooped up some sand and knelt down to form a square at the base of the tree.

"Mom, I'm tired of this," Alex whined.

"Just a little longer. Then we can all go get pie and hot chocolate." She added a ribbon and a bow.

"I'm going back to town. All my friends are probably playing at the park by now." He ran off toward the stairs.

"Alex, get back here," Maggie called. She and Jake jogged over to the stairs to catch up with him, but it only made him go faster, taking the steps two at a time without holding on to the railing. When he was only ten feet in front of them, Jake watched in horror as he slipped on a patch of ice and crashed down to the step, landing on his left arm.

"Owie, owie." Tears streamed down Alex's face as he cradled his arm. Maggie was at his side in a second.

"Are you okay? Can you move it? I told you not to run on the stairs." She touched his arm and he winced. She shook her head. "They should have put sand on the stairs. Someone could have broken their neck."

His arm hung at his side at an awkward angle. Alex tried unsuccessfully to rotate his arm.

Jake knelt by his nephew and inspected the injury. "Yep, I'd say that was broken."

Alex burst out into a fresh torrent of tears. "Now I can't ride my bike."

Jake smiled. "You'll be okay in a few weeks. They'll put a cast on your arm and you'll be good as new."

Maggie turned to Jake. "What do we do? He's never broken a bone before."

"His pediatrician should be able to set it."

Her face fell. "It's Saturday, they won't be in."

"Okay, well, let's take him to the hospital in Haven Shores." They helped Alex to a standing position. Slowly, they made their way to the car. Tears were bright in Alex's eyes and Maggie cringed whenever his face twisted in pain.

Jake put his arm around Maggie, who looked like she was about to cry herself. "Boys break bones, it'll be okay. It's part of growing up. Did Brian ever tell you about breaking his leg falling out of a tree when he was a kid?"

"No, never." Maggie looked at him with interest as they helped Alex into the car and carefully strapped him into his booster seat. "What was he doing?"

Jake looked at Alex in the rearview mirror as he related the story. "Well, you see, your father bet me that he could get an apple from the top of the tree in Grandma and Grandpa's backyard. Have you seen that tree?"

Alex nodded. "It's huge."

Jake smiled. "It is very tall. Your dad picked out an apple near the very top to be his goal. He actually did make it to the top, but when he tried to carry his prize apple down, his foot slipped off a branch and he toppled out of the tree. I was standing below him, but there was nothing I could do. He was down there on the ground, with the bone sticking out of his skin and blood everywhere."

"Ew," Alex said. "That sounds gross. At least the bone isn't sticking out of my skin."

Maggie made a face and turned a little green. "I can't

believe he never told me about this. I always wondered how he got that scar on his leg, but I never asked."

"Yeah, and of course, I got blamed for it. I was the older brother and according to my mom, I should have been more careful." He glanced at Maggie. "But you know Brian, he was headstrong and ready for any challenge that came along. There was no way I could talk him out of climbing that tree once he'd set his mind on it."

Maggie laughed. "That does sound like Brian. I remember trying to talk him out of climbing out on a ledge one time when we were hiking. He scared me so badly that I refused to talk to him until we had reached the trailhead."

Alex piped up. "Tell me more about my dad, Uncle Jake."

The rest of the way to Haven Shores, Jake regaled them with stories of his younger brother. It felt right telling Maggie and Alex his memories of Brian, almost cathartic in a way. He and his brother hadn't been close in later years as their jobs took over their lives and moved them across the world from each other, but when they were kids, they'd played together often, even with a five-year age difference.

They arrived at the hospital in Haven Shores and the emergency room staff had Alex's arm immobilized in a cast in no time. Maggie was still shaken up over the accident, so after they had Alex settled in his seat, Jake held open the passenger side door for her. She paused next to the door.

He smiled at her. "See, I told you it was no big deal."

"I'm glad you were here. I don't know what I would have done if I were by myself. I really hate it when he gets hurt." She surprised him by leaning in to hug him. He wrapped his arms around her and patted her back before he reluctantly released her. Although she was hugging him out of worry and relief, he'd take what he could get.

"I'm glad I was here too, and happy that he wasn't hurt worse."

She nodded, smiled gratefully at him, and got into the car. He shut her door and whistled as he walked around to the driver's side. While he hated seeing his nephew injured, it felt good to be able to help Maggie and her son as he'd promised to his brother.

10

The next morning, Maggie looked up from her laptop and shouted down the hall. "Alex! Are you okay in there?" He'd been in the bathroom for ten minutes already.

"Yeah. It's hard to wash my hands with the cast on my arm."

"You know, if you hadn't run away, you wouldn't have broken your arm." An icy chill ran up her spine as the image of her little boy slipping on the steps played out in her mind in slow motion. She shuddered. It could have been so much worse.

"I know, Mom," he shouted back.

She returned to her computer screen. Velma's rant about the size of the party room at the café had been on her mind. With more and more tourists holding large functions in town, the side room simply wasn't big enough to host those events. The town lacked an event center and desperately needed one. If there was someplace to hold events, more people would want to have weddings, reunions and maybe even conferences in Candle Beach. It would be good for the whole town—and her startup catering business in particular. She'd hoped to partner with someone who owned an existing space.

But so far, every proprietor she'd contacted either wasn't interested in a catering arrangement with her or didn't want to have their space used for events. However, there was one property online that had caught her eye.

"Hey, Alex," she called out. She waited a moment and then said, "Are you ready to go?"

The bathroom door banged open and his footsteps sounded in the hall. "I'm ready. This cast is itchy though." He banged it into the living room wall carelessly as he walked past, scuffing the paint.

"Alex!" she chided, but didn't discipline him. Chipped paint wasn't anything to lose sleep over. With an active growing boy, she expected her apartment to get banged up. She grabbed her purse and turned off the lights. "Let's go. I promised Gretchen we'd meet her at her office at one o'clock."

"Okay, okay," he grumbled, but he got into the car nicely.

Maggie parked in her reserved space behind the café and they walked the few blocks to Candle Beach Real Estate. Gretchen greeted them at the door. "I saw you walk past the window." She motioned to a bench along the wall with a coffee table in front of it. "Alex, you can go play over there while your mom and I talk. There's a kids' tablet and some Legos in a basket under the coffee table."

"Yay! Thanks, Ms. Gretchen." He scurried over to the play area.

Gretchen turned to Maggie. "Do you want coffee? I made a fresh pot when I got in today. I'm dragging this afternoon and could really use another cup."

She nodded. "Me too. Yesterday wore me out with Alex's visit to the emergency room."

"Yeah, I saw the cast. What happened?"

"He slipped on the beach access stairs after we built a sand sculpture for the winter festival."

"Ouch." Gretchen grimaced. "Poor kid. At least he'll have fun tomorrow at school when his friends ask to sign his cast."

They grabbed mugs of coffee and she led Maggie back to her desk. Just the scent of the coffee invigorated Maggie, as though she had absorbed some of the caffeine through the air.

"Thanks for meeting me today. I appreciate you coming in on a Sunday."

"No problem, real estate never sleeps." Gretchen grinned and pulled something up on her computer.

"So you're interested in the Sorensen farm." She gave Maggie a questioning look. "What do you want with a farm? You've never mentioned any interest in agriculture. Is this some new farm-to-table initiative at the Bluebonnet Café?"

Maggie laughed. "No, but that's a really good idea. I'll think about that." She sobered. "This might sound crazy, but I was thinking about possibly buying the Sorensen place to use as an event center. You know how little event space there is in Candle Beach." She peeked at her friend from behind her coffee cup.

Gretchen appeared thoughtful. "No, I don't think it's crazy, but it would be a lot of work. Are you thinking of using the barn as the main event space?"

"Yeah." Maggie felt her spirits rise with her friend's positive response. "I'd turn the barn into a lovely event space and then maybe rent the house out. From the pictures, it looks like there's plenty of parking in front of the barn. I'm not sure what to do about bathrooms, but I'd figure it out. And that view of Bluebonnet Lake—it's to die for and would be a huge draw for customers. We could even put a deck in overlooking the lake for ceremonies." The ideas just bubbled out until she noticed Gretchen staring at her. "Well, maybe not everything at once," she added sheepishly.

"Uh-huh." Her friend smiled. "I'm asking as your real estate agent now and not your friend, but can you afford it? With the house and land, the property isn't cheap."

Maggie's spirits deflated. Usually she was so pragmatic, but something about this idea made her lose her practicality. "I think I can swing it. The café is doing well and I know I can earn enough from catering the events to make it profitable. But, of course, I still have to convince the bank of that."

Gretchen smiled. "I'm sure you won't have any problem. If I know you, you'll have a business plan created by tomorrow to wow the banker."

Her face flushed. "I'm already halfway through with my business plan."

Gretchen laughed. "Okay, then. You haven't seen the property yet, right?"

"No, only pictures. I was hoping you might have time to take me to look at it tomorrow? Pretty please?" Maggie tried to give Gretchen her most convincing expression.

"Of course." Gretchen clicked on the calendar on her computer. "I can do an early afternoon appointment. Maybe two o'clock? Does that work?"

"Yes, thanks, Gretch." She glanced at her watch. "I've got to get Alex home. The babysitter is coming over soon because I promised one of my waitresses I'd cover her shift tonight." She signaled to her son from across the room, but couldn't get his attention.

"I'll have to tear him away from that tablet." She grinned at Gretchen. "I'll see you tomorrow."

Gretchen nodded and went back to working on her computer.

~

Monday morning, Jake arrived at Maggie's apartment to take Alex to school. She had a morning shift at the café and he'd jumped at the chance to spend more time with his nephew. When he got there, he pushed open the unlocked door and found her sitting at the kitchen table, drinking coffee with a pained expression on her face.

"Your door was unlocked."

"I know. I just unlocked it for you, Mr. Police Officer," she teased. "I didn't know if I'd be out of the shower when you got here. And Alex and I don't seem to be on speaking terms today, so he certainly wouldn't have told me if you knocked on the door."

He opted against making the safety speech and cocked his head to the side. "What's going on with him?"

"Beats me," she said. "He's been in his room all morning. He's upset about something and doesn't want to talk to me about it. I don't know what's gotten into him. He used to be such a sweet kid all the time. Now he's so moody." She sighed. "A year ago, he never would have run away from us like he did at the festival."

Jake shrugged. "He's growing up and trying to assert his independence. Maybe not in the most constructive way, but you can't expect him to stay your baby forever."

His words hit her the wrong way. "You're giving me parenting advice?"

He held up his hands. "No, not at all. I didn't mean it

that way. I just mean all kids grow up." He added more gently, "Is it okay if I talk to him?"

She motioned to his room. "Be my guest."

Jake poked his head into his nephew's room. "Hey, Alex, I'm here to take you to school." Maggie was right. He didn't have much parenting experience, but he had a suspicion his nephew was upset about something and didn't want to tell his mom. So what was it?

"Cool." Alex lay on his bed, staring up at the ceiling. The word was upbeat, but his face was glum.

"What's wrong?" Jake sat down next to him on the bed and the boy scooted himself up to sit against the wall behind his bed.

"It's this dumb thing." He frowned at the offending object that immobilized his arm. "How am I supposed to play kickball with my friends at recess? This cast gets in the way."

Was that all? Jake sighed inwardly. He put his arm around Alex. "It won't be on for long. Besides, think of how much fun it will be to have all of your friends sign your cast."

"Yeah!" Alex brightened. "Do you have a pen? Can you sign it?"

Jake grinned. "I'll see what your mom has for pens." He stood from the bed and started to walk toward the door.

"No." Alex said sharply.

Jake swiveled around. "What's wrong?"

"She's so mad at me for running away and falling on the steps." He hung his head. "I know it was a dumb move, but I didn't want to be down on the beach any longer. All my friends were up playing in the park already."

"So you think your mom will be mad if you mention the cast?"

"Yeah. She gets upset every time I mention anything about it. And she's looking at a farm or something today. I don't want to make her mad."

Jake nodded. "I'll talk with her."

Alex looked relieved. "Thanks, Uncle Jake."

Jake left his nephew's room and walked down the hall to the kitchen.

~

"How's he doing?" Maggie asked from where she stood washing dishes at the kitchen sink.

"Well, he's worried that you're mad at him about running away and falling on the ice, so he doesn't want to tell you how much the cast bothers him."

"He's right about that. I hate thinking about how bad his fall could have been." She shivered. "But what do you mean it bothers him? Is his arm hurting? Should I take him back in to the doctor?"

"Whoa, ease up there. He's fine. Just a little self-conscious of the cast and worried about how it will affect his ball-playing abilities."

"Oh." She put a cup in the dishwasher. "Is there anything I can do? He's always come to me about his problems before."

"No, he'll survive. I convinced him the cast was an asset."

She raised an eyebrow. "An asset?"

"Yeah, his friends will think he's really cool when they get to sign his cast. Do you have a permanent marker I could use to sign it? I promised him I'd check with you."

She smiled. "Ah. I get it. Thanks for doing this, Jake. I appreciate all your help. With my parents gone, I couldn't have done it without you."

"No problem." He flashed her an easy grin. "I love helping with Alex. He's my nephew, after all." He eyed her. "Alex mentioned you were looking at a farm property nearby today. Are you planning to move?"

She laughed. "No, I have this crazy idea that it would make an awesome events center. I don't know if you've noticed, but there aren't many big spaces for gatherings in this town. I don't know if this particular location is the right place for me to buy, but it doesn't hurt to start looking."

"Ah. That makes sense." He picked a pen out of a jar on the counter and spun it between his fingers. "If you need another opinion on the farm property, let me know."

She nodded, and Jake sauntered down the hall to Alex's room, pen in hand. Watching him walk away, she was suddenly filled with a surge of love for him. She'd been at a loss about what to do with Alex and he'd figured out the problem quickly. He'd rapidly become a big part of their lives, and she wasn't sure what they'd do without him.

Should she tell him she had feelings for him though? It seemed like every time she was around him now her stomach got all topsy-turvy and her brain turned to mush. If things were this bad and they weren't even dating, how would it be if they were officially in a romantic relationship? She couldn't afford to not be at the top of her game.

Jake's deep, reassuring voice floated down the hall from Alex's room. She didn't want to mess things up for Alex, and with everything going on with Dahlia's wedding and the catering business, this wasn't the best time to start dating. After the New Year, things would be settled and she would reconsider dating Jake or the idea of dating in general.

11

"Thanks for agreeing to tour the farm property with me." Maggie shifted in the driver's seat of her car and glanced at Jake.

He flashed her a smile. "Of course. I'd love to see the place you're considering."

They pulled up in front of the farmhouse overlooking Bluebonnet Lake.

"Gretchen is going to meet us here." She motioned to the property and the lake below. "Isn't it beautiful?"

The lake drew his attention first. Blue-green waters lapped lazily at the shoreline. Just off shore, a man wearing a khaki fishing hat had his line in the water, ready to pull in the big one. It was a picture-perfect small-town lake.

He looked away from the lake and focused on the barn. The pictures on the online listing had made it look inhabitable, but in real life it appeared to be held up by bits of hay and dust. The farmhouse itself was a charming yellow Craftsman with white shutters and had been kept up. Flower boxes hung from the windows, although nothing grew in them. Fields surrounded the farmhouse and barn, the dirt barren and gloomy in the dead of winter. Muddy ruts covered the ground between the barn and house.

"I'm sure it will work out well." He wasn't sure how she'd pull it off, but he knew anything was possible with Maggie. And maybe the barn's interior was in better repair than the outside.

She traipsed over to the barn wearing black boots covered with cute yellow ducks. He hung back a few steps behind her and couldn't help but check her out as she picked her way between mud puddles. Even dressed in a raincoat and boots, she was beautiful. When they reached the barn, she turned to him, her face glowing with enthusiasm.

"I can't wait until you see the inside. The floor space is huge. It'll be perfect for ceremonies and parties."

A car pulled up and Gretchen exited. She waved and strode over to them in rubber boots of her own. "Got my appropriate footwear." She lifted her foot. "I don't think my tan pumps will ever come clean from visiting this place on Monday."

Maggie frowned. "Sorry about that."

Gretchen flicked her hand in the air. "That's a hazard of my job. I've lost many pairs of shoes over the years. Don't even worry about it." She gestured to the barn and turned to Jake. "What do you think so far?"

"Uh, it's rustic." He tried to keep his tone enthusiastic, but wasn't sure if he'd succeeded.

Gretchen unlocked the padlock as Maggie stood at the door, bouncing on the balls of her feet, ready to release the door handle. As soon as the lock clicked she flung the door open. The odor of dusty hay assaulted Jake. He hung back, letting fresh air enter the barn. Maggie went inside first, her words bubbling out faster than he could understand.

His first impression had been overly optimistic. Inside the barn, the rafters were covered in cobwebs and hay bales were stacked ten high in the corner. The wood partitions in the area where the farmer had thrown hay down to the cows were broken and hanging haphazardly.

"See how great it is?" Maggie spun around, scanning the barn.

"Um, it's a large space for events. I'm sure it will be great when you get it fixed up." He couldn't figure out how even Maggie could get this mess cleaned up and turned into a space that other people would pay large sums of money to rent.

She grabbed his hand. He looked at her in surprise, but she didn't seem to notice his reaction. He smiled slightly and allowed her to lead him over to a corner of the barn. Gretchen hung back by the door then went outside when her phone rang.

"Look. This is where I'll put the bar. And then in the front, we can have the DJ or even a live band. There's plenty of room." She pulled him toward the back wall and let go of his hand to motion toward the full span of the barn.

"Close your eyes," she ordered.

He closed them dutifully.

She put her hand on his arm and said, "Now, imagine a small stage here for a wedding. The wedding party stands here on either side of you. In front of you are all the wedding guests. And then your bride walks down the aisle toward you."

In a flash, he could see everything she said. With the walls cleaned up and whitewashed, the space would be light and airy, with the high windows letting in plenty of light. He imagined the buzz of the crowd and then the sound of the wedding march. He shivered.

He'd never thought too seriously about his wedding before, but now he could see it as clear as day. In his vision, the barn doors opened, and there was his bride, illuminated by the sunlight behind her. She walked toward him, her curly red hair shimmering below the veil. When she reached him, she touched his arm. He opened his eyes. Maggie stood before him, not wearing a wedding dress, but looking as beautiful as she had in his vision.

He breathed in sharply. His daydream had been so clear. He focused in on her face. She smiled at him now, with an expression of joy.

"Isn't it beautiful?"

"Yes, yes it is." Her face glowed and he knew in that instant that he wanted to marry her and be a father to Alex. Was there any chance she felt the same? Was he being crazy and this was guilt over not taking care of them earlier? What would Brian think?

"I've got to get some fresh air. I think the hay is bothering my sinuses." He coughed for emphasis. Maggie nodded and continued to pace the room, probably plotting where each dining table would be placed.

He walked past Gretchen in the doorway, who looked at him with a knowing smile. She joined him outside.

"You've got a thing for Maggie, don't you?" She wore a mischievous smile.

"Is it that obvious?" He toed the dirt and then looked her in the eye.

"Well, if that dreamy expression on your face whenever she touches you is any indication, you've got it bad."

He grimaced. "Do you think she knows?"

"She has so much on her mind right now, I don't really

know. What are your intentions though? Are you planning on staying in Candle Beach? Maggie shouldn't have to be disappointed by any man after what she's gone through."

"I agree. And I have no intention of starting anything with her that I can't follow through on." A thrill of excitement rose up from his stomach, paralyzing his throat for a moment. Was he committing to asking Maggie out?

Gretchen smiled and nodded. "Good. Maggie needs someone in her life that will care about her and Alex. I think you could be that person."

"I hope so."

He heard footsteps behind him.

"What are you two gabbing about out here?" Maggie picked a piece of hay out of her hair and twisted it in her fingers before tossing it on the ground.

"Oh, we were just discussing the history of this property," Gretchen said innocently. "Jake was fascinated by the fact that this farm was one of the first settlements in the area."

"Oh. Yes, that's one of the things I love about it. I think customers will be interested in the history as well." Maggie sounded giddy with excitement. She grabbed Jake's arm again and Gretchen winked at him.

"Did you two want to see the farmhouse?"

He checked his watch. "I have a little more time. Let's do it."

The entered the house and Jake was more assured of the investment. The inside of the house's condition matched the outside. It wouldn't take much to make it livable.

"I like it." He ran his hands over the wooden railing leading to the upstairs. It was solid, the way houses used to be constructed. The house was simple—three bedrooms and a bathroom upstairs and a living room, kitchen and bathroom downstairs. "Would you want to live here?"

Maggie shook her head. "No, it's too big for just Alex and me. I thought I'd rent it out nightly, either to guests at the events or in the Candle Beach nightly rental pool."

They exited the house and Gretchen locked the door.

"I've got to get back to the office, Maggie. Let me know if you want to put an offer in on the property."

"Thanks, Gretchen. I need to think about it for a while." She turned to Jake. "You think it's a good business investment, right?"

He turned away from the farmhouse and viewed the barn again. It hadn't gotten any better looking. He didn't want to lie to her, but he didn't want to shatter her dreams either.

"It could be beautiful, but it will take a lot of work—and money. Do you want to take this on with everything else in your life?"

She stared at him. "I thought you'd be more supportive."

"Maggie, I am, but I don't want you to take too much on. You have the café and Alex. That's a lot for anyone."

She bristled visibly. "I know I have a lot of responsibilities. Don't tell me I'm not making Alex a priority."

He tried to touch her arm, but she brushed him away. He held his hand up in the air. "I'm not. I'd better be getting back to work now anyway. I think my lunch break is over."

"Fine." Maggie drove them the few minutes back to town in silence and dropped him off at the police station.

"I'll see you later this week, okay? I promised Alex I'd play a board game with him."

"Sure. I'll see you then." She drove off, leaving him wondering how everything had soured so quickly.

~

Maggie surveyed the side room at the Bluebonnet Café. It seated thirty if you really squished people into the small space. For Dahlia's rehearsal dinner, that was what would need to happen if they wanted everyone to fit. She sat down at one of the tables with her notebook, ready to go over her lists for the party. The wedding couple would sit at the head of the table, with their parents on either side of them. Maggie and Gretchen would be at the other table with Garrett's groomsmen, his best friends from college.

She frowned. The space was really tight. Candle Beach desperately needed an events space. Dahlia's wedding would be held in heated tents on the Marina Park grounds, but that was expensive and less than ideal for most gatherings.

Was the old Sorensen farm the right venue though? It had potential, but Jake was right—it needed a lot of work. She'd never been afraid of hard work before, but with Alex and the café, she'd be overextended.

Who was she kidding? She'd arrived at her breaking point a long time ago and had somehow clung to the precipice. On one hand, it felt right to branch out from the catering business and have a venue to use for events. On the other hand, there were so many reasons not to buy the property. It would be expensive. She'd be tapped out on savings. It would be a huge risk.

She was usually risk averse, but this seemed like something the town could really use. And it could bring in more tourists, which would benefit everyone in the long run. It wouldn't hurt to see what the bank said about a loan.

At lunchtime, she stopped off at the bank. She pushed the door open and inhaled the smell of paper and money, a scent she'd loved since her mother took her there to open her first savings account when she was five.

Lars Johnson, the bank manager, wasn't busy and immediately ushered her over to his desk. "Ah, the old Sorensen farm. I remember when they had horses out there. We used to go riding with the Sorensen kids." He smiled as he reminisced about the good old days.

"I want to make it into a premier location for wedding receptions, reunions, and the like. You know Candle Beach needs something like this."

"Yes, it does. I completely agree." He folded his hands in front of him on the desk. "So what type of loan amount are you looking for?"

Maggie told him the amount she needed. She lifted her bag and pulled out a folder with the business proposal she'd finished that morning. She pushed it towards him. "As you see, I'm projecting one hundred percent capacity on summer weekends and about fifty percent for winter weekends, not to mention the weekday events we'd have. I've been hosting events at the café, but demand is exceeding what I can provide."

"I see." He reviewed the stapled pages, then tapped some numbers into his computer and frowned.

"I'm sorry, Maggie, but while we can offer you a loan to purchase the property, the interest rate isn't optimal. Unless...do you have anything you can use as collateral?"

Her heart sank. She didn't own a house or anything. The only thing of value that she owned was the Bluebonnet Café. Bile rose up from her stomach. Was it worth mortgaging the café?

"I might be able to get some collateral for a loan. Can I think on it?"

"Sure, Maggie. Let me know when you decide. I know whatever you try, though, you'll succeed."

Maggie smiled. "Thanks, Lars."

She exited the bank deep in thought. Losing the Bluebonnet Café wasn't an option. She couldn't risk it, but she didn't want to give up on her dream either. Buying the farm property wasn't a decision she could make on a whim.

12

*T*he day of Dahlia's rehearsal dinner came quickly.

"Maggie, this is lovely," Dahlia's mother Vanessa said, gesturing to the long dining table in the side room of the cafe. "Those flower arrangements are gorgeous."

"And the food is amazing." Garrett came up from behind Vanessa and shook Maggie's hand. "Again, Maggie, thanks for doing this."

"You're welcome." She smiled. This was why she loved the hospitality industry. Her efforts paid off in happy customers.

"How are arrangements for the wedding tents going?" she asked Garrett.

"Not as well as I'd like. I had to get permits from the town to put up the tents in the Marina Park and there was a snafu in the permit process." He frowned. "But I think we finally got everything worked out."

"Good." She straightened a pitcher of water on a nearby serving cart.

He regarded her critically. "Have you ever thought about opening your own place to host events? You'd be good at it."

She laughed. "Actually, I toured a place yesterday. I'm not sure about it though. It was expensive and would be a lot of work."

"I'm sure you'll figure it out." He winked at her and waved at someone across the room. "I've got to go say hi to Dahlia's cousin. Her little boy is going to be our ring bearer."

Maggie edged toward the kitchen, more focused on her role as café owner than bridesmaid.

Then a loud crash and gasps came from inside the party room. She rushed back in to see what the commotion was about. Velma stood at the side of the room, holding an empty tray, her face sullen. Glass shards and soda pop intermixed on the floor and a sweet smell filled the air. One of the guests was dabbing at her pants and the rest were trying studiously to ignore the mess. Maggie smiled at them and then turned to her employee.

"What happened?" she asked, not sure she wanted to hear the answer.

"What happened?" Velma gave her an incredulous look. "Someone moved their chair out as I was passing by with a full tray of drinks." She glared at the poor woman with the stained pantsuit. "I told you this was going to happen."

"You weren't even scheduled to help in here. What happened to Lily?" After Velma's rant about the party room's size, Maggie had made sure to keep her out of there for Dahlia's rehearsal dinner.

"Lily went on break. Someone had to cover for her." Velma glared at her now.

Maggie closed her eyes for a brief second before taking charge.

"Okay. Please go back to your regular tables. I'll have

someone clean this up." She brushed the mess aside with a napkin as best as she could. Velma huffed at her and left the room.

She approached the woman with the stained pants. "I'm so sorry about this. I'll get you some club soda for that, alright?"

The woman nodded gratefully. Maggie returned to the kitchen and instructed one of the busboys to clean up the broken glass, then brought some club soda and another type of stain remover back to the woman.

"The bathroom is that way. Let me know if you need anything else." The woman nodded.

The mess was soon taken care of and the party guests seemed happy to be there. Maggie couldn't help hovering around the fringes, ready to manage any potential crisis that popped up.

Gretchen tapped her on the shoulder. "Relax. Your staff has this. You should have a little fun—enjoy yourself."

Maggie looked around. "There's so much to do though. Did you see what happened with the spilled drinks?"

Gretchen laughed. "Those things happen. Trust your staff. If you want to open an events venue, you're going to need to let go of things at the café a little."

Maggie forced herself to relax. "I guess so," she said reluctantly. Gretchen gave her a little wave and walked back to join her boyfriend Parker at their table.

A waitress carrying a tray of drinks came by and smiled at her. She watched anxiously as the woman handed each customer their drink.

Dahlia came over and hugged her. Her face was flushed and she handed Maggie a glass of white wine.

"This is great. Everyone loved their entrees."

"Thanks."

"Gretchen mentioned you were thinking about buying a farm to host events. Is that the one overlooking Bluebonnet Lake?"

She nodded. "It is. It comes with a farmhouse and a barn, which is what I would use for the events space." She frowned. "But it's so expensive. I'm not sure I can afford it without jeopardizing the café."

"Can you get an investor?" Dahlia asked.

"I thought about that, but I want to have control over the space. If I rent out the farmhouse, I may be able to make it work." She forced herself to smile. "Enough about me. I heard from Garrett that your tents are ready to set up. Your wedding is going to be beautiful."

"I hope so. I constantly think about how nice it would have been to elope and not have to worry about any of this other stuff."

Maggie laughed. "Believe me, I get it. For my wedding, I had three binders full of contact information, charts and lists."

Dahlia made a face. "I haven't gone quite that far, but I do feel pretty organized." A proud smile crossed her face. "And I think you should go for the events center if you can. I've noticed an increase in tourist traffic, so I think you could make a success of it. What does Jake think?"

"Why would it matter what Jake thinks?" Maggie asked testily.

"I thought you said he was going to see the farm too."

"Yeah, and he doesn't think I can make it work."

"Hmm." Dahlia sipped her wine and eyed Maggie.

"I think your mom is calling out for you." Maggie pointed at Vanessa, who was waving at her daughter from across the room.

Dahlia hugged her again and whispered in her ear, "If anyone can do it, you can."

Maggie nodded, but she now felt more conflicted than ever.

~

Two days later, Maggie was in a tizzy trying to finish preparations for Dahlia's wedding. A crew from the rental company had set up two large tents in the Marina Park. One contained rows of white wooden chairs and a stage for the ceremony. After the nuptials, they'd clear the chairs off to the side to allow room for dancing.

The other had been set up with round tables and chairs. Long tables for the buffet lined one side of the tent. The supplier had made good on their promise to bring the additional quantities for her order and her staff at the café had been up since five a.m. preparing the food. So far, everything had gone off without a hitch.

Jake was watching Alex, so she didn't have to worry about a babysitter. She'd invited him to be her date to Dahlia's wedding before they'd toured the barn together. She'd thought she'd felt something brewing romantically between them, but now she didn't know if she'd imagined it. Tonight would be interesting, that was for sure.

A few hours later, Dahlia, Gretchen, and Maggie gathered together at Dahlia's house to get ready for the big day. Dani at Candle Beach Cuts had done Dahlia's hair in an ornate bridal updo.

"Your hair looks gorgeous." Maggie admired the tiny pearls threaded through Dahlia's auburn hair.

"Thanks, I was pretty happy with it too." Dahlia applied

mascara and blusher and viewed herself in the mirror before turning around. "What do you girls think?"

"You look beautiful," Gretchen said. "That dress looks even more perfect today than it did when you had your fittings."

Maggie leaned over Dahlia's voluminous wedding dress and hugged her.

"And I love our bridesmaid dresses." The violet dresses Dahlia had chosen were comfortable and stylish, something Maggie appreciated.

Someone knocked on the door. "Honey, are you decent?" Vanessa called out.

"Yeah, Mom. Come on in."

Vanessa pushed the door open and came in, then closed it behind her. "Oh, honey." Tears slipped out of her eyes.

"Mom, you're going to make me cry." Dahlia swiped at her own eyes with a Kleenex.

Maggie and Gretchen exchanged glances. "We'll leave you two alone." Maggie stood. "I've got to go check on some things for the reception."

Dahlia waved goodbye to them.

The round tables were set up and her staff had already covered them with white tablecloths. One-third of them had been set with violet napkins encircled with silver-hued napkin rings, and her crew was placing pitchers of water on each table.

Lindsay, her lead server for the catering business, approached her. "Maggie, we don't have enough silverware."

Maggie stared at her. How could they possibly not have enough silverware?

"What do you mean? I ordered new sets for the catering business. There should have been at least 150 place settings.

I checked them off when they arrived in the latest shipment."

"The box said 150, but there were only fifty sets in there."

Maggie closed her eyes for a moment. "Fifty? So we're short one hundred sets?"

Lindsay squirmed. "Sorry, Maggie. I can see if we can spare any from the café."

"Thanks. Let me know what you find out and I'll try to think of something." She stared at the empty tables. Where the heck was she going to get one hundred sets of silverware from in the next two hours? There wasn't time to drive to Haven Shores to purchase more, even if they had that many sets available at the stores. She could wrangle some from the café, but it was a Saturday night and they'd need most of their silverware.

She called every eating establishment in town, but they all had the same predicament—not enough to share.

Then she called Jake to ask if he'd take Alex to the B&B with him when he went back to get dressed for the wedding.

"Sure, I can do that. But, I thought you were coming back to finish getting dressed."

"I can't. I had my dress here and I have a mini crisis on my hands." Her stress levels were increasing.

"What's going on?"

She sighed. "There was an error in my order of silverware and we didn't notice it until now. Totally my fault. I should have checked the box to confirm we'd received them all. The end result is that I'm short one hundred sets of silverware. Do you think Dahlia will notice if we use plastic forks?" She laughed, but it didn't break her bad feeling.

"Uh..." Jake paused. "I'm pretty sure she'd notice."

"Yeah, I figured so. I'm hoping I can find some regular silverware before the ceremony, but it's not looking good."

At an hour to go, she was about to admit defeat and use white plastic picnicware. She grimaced. It would look so bad to use plastic utensils for her first real event. But it would be better than having the guests eat with their fingers.

She saw Jake and Alex enter the tent area and waved at them. They were still dressed in their regular clothes. "What are you guys doing here?"

"I found something for you." Jake opened a shoebox and showed her the contents. "Will these work?"

Her eyes widened. The cardboard box contained about twenty sets of silverware. "Yeah, those are great, but I'm going to need a lot more." Still, it gave her hope they could find more before the reception dinner.

"I've got them. I have three more boxes just like this in my car. Probably about eighty total place settings."

She threw her arms around him and then looked into his eyes. "You're kidding!"

He grinned at her and shook his head.

"Where did you get these?"

"Well, you know the B&B I'm staying at?" He closed the box lid.

"Uh-huh." Where was he going with this? Why would a B&B have eighty sets of nice tableware?

"The owner, Maude, used to own an Italian restaurant in Haven Shores. When she sold the business, the new owner didn't want her supplies, so she has a whole closet full of plates, linen napkins, tablecloths and silverware. She thought she might want to open another restaurant some-day, so she didn't sell them."

Maggie's mouth gaped open. "How did you know about all the restaurant supplies?"

He shrugged. "She has arthritis and can't climb ladders very well. She needed me to get something down from the top of the closet one time." He looked at her. "So will they work?"

"Yes, yes, thank you. You're a lifesaver." She hugged him again, a warmth passing between them. "I can get twenty sets from the café. They'll just have to wash silverware quickly tonight."

She called Lindsay over and instructed her to have the crew get the other utensils out of Jake's car and take them to be washed at the café.

"I'll see you at the ceremony, okay?" Maggie said to Jake and Alex. They nodded.

"Hey, Mom, you look really pretty." Alex smiled at her.

She kissed his head. "Thanks, honey."

The two of them walked off hand in hand. She watched them for a minute, happy to see how well they were getting along, and then sprung into action on last-minute reception details.

13

Maggie walked down the aisle with one of Garrett's groomsmen and joined Gretchen on one side of the stage. Garrett stood in the center of the raised platform, his face a mixture of anxiety and excitement. She smiled at him, but he was too focused on the closed tent flaps to notice.

Then the wedding march sounded and Dahlia came through the tent door. All eyes turned to her and the guests stood as she walked by. Dahlia's knuckles were white as she gripped her bouquet, but her eyes held nothing but love. The groom seemed mesmerized by his bride, not taking his eyes off of her until she had joined him on the small stage.

They said their vows and the love and warmth they shared for each other was obvious. Many of the guests dabbed at their eyes as they watched the ceremony, Maggie included. She shot a glance at Jake sitting in the audience with Alex. Would she ever marry again? A few weeks ago, she would have said it was unlikely, but now she didn't know.

The officiant declared them husband and wife, and

Garrett pulled Dahlia in for a long kiss. The audience cheered and the newly married couple parted and punched the air while beaming a matching pair of thousand-watt grins. They bounced down the aisle toward the tent door and the bridal party followed at a more sedate pace. Outside, Maggie had to chuckle when she spotted Dahlia and Garrett kissing behind the ceremony tent as she entered the other tent to check on the buffet preparations.

The inside of the dining tent was gorgeous. Her staff had hung twinkly white lights from the rafters and jazz music played softly in the background.

They'd filled chafing dishes with salmon, chicken cordon bleu and tender filets of beef. Her stomach grumbled to remind her she'd skipped lunch to take care of wedding preparations. Further down the line, chive-topped mashed potatoes, a green salad, and miscellaneous other side dishes awaited the wedding guests.

"What do you think?" Lindsay wore a proud smile.

"You guys have done a great job." Gretchen had been right. She could count on her staff to take care of things when she wasn't available.

"Hey, I think the reception line is forming. You'd better get out there."

"Thanks." Maggie smiled at her and exited the tent.

Sure enough, Dahlia and Garrett had lined up against one side of the tent and were greeting guests. Maggie squeezed into the line between Gretchen and one of the groomsmen.

"Sorry I'm late, I was checking on things," she whispered to Gretchen.

"I figured that," Gretchen whispered back. "Don't worry, you haven't missed much."

Maggie shook hands and made small talk with each

guest as they waited to give their regards to the wedding couple.

When the last guest had cycled through, she joined Alex and Jake at the table Dahlia had assigned to the bridal party. She and Garrett sat at a small table at the front by themselves.

Jake stood as she approached the table and held out her chair for her. Gretchen and Parker sat down across from them, along with the groomsmen and their significant others.

"Everything looks wonderful. Your event is a success."

"I hope so." She smiled at him and held up a spoon. "Thanks to you, we're not eating off white plastic."

"No problem." He gave her an easy grin. "Now let's go eat. It's time for you to be a party guest." He motioned to their tablemates who had already risen and entered the buffet line. Alex tugged at her arm.

"C'mon, Mom, I'm so hungry."

Maggie allowed him to drag her over to the buffet line, although she found herself gazing longingly at the staff area, wanting to know how everything was going. In the line, she overheard people commenting on how good the food looked and smelled and her chest puffed out a little.

After they ate, she and others regaled the crowd with tales about Dahlia and Garrett. She found herself tearing up at the way they looked at each other as their friends spoke of the love between them. The guests toasted the newly married couple then everyone moved to the other tent. The staff had decorated it much like the first, with white and violet lights hanging from the rafters and doorways. The overall effect was magical.

Alex ran off as soon as they arrived to play with a friend who had attended the wedding with his parents. Then

Dahlia and Garrett danced the first dance. She watched her friend swirl effortlessly across the floor in her new husband's arms and wished for the same happiness for herself. The band changed to a faster song and the couple left the floor, laughing as they held hands.

Jake rested his hand on her shoulder, breaking her out of her reverie. "Do you want to dance?"

She checked on Alex, who was playing happily on the other side of the huge tent. "Sure, I'd love to." Back in the day, she'd loved to dance, but now, other than dancing in front of her bathroom mirror, she didn't have much opportunity to do so.

They danced about a foot apart and she felt herself relax as they moved to the beat. Then the fast song ended and a slow number came over the speakers.

He held his hand out to her and she took it. He drew her close to his chest and she felt herself relax against him. Somehow, being with him made her feel safe and sure that everything was right in the world.

"I didn't have a chance to tell you earlier how beautiful you look in that dress." Jake lifted his hand from her waist and brushed a lock of hair away from her face. His touch felt fantastic and she closed her eyes to savor the feeling.

"Thank you. You clean up nice too."

He wore a gray suit with a dark navy-blue button-down shirt and gray patterned tie. Normally, he wore jeans and a T-shirt, which she didn't object to, but dressed for the occasion, he looked amazingly handsome.

They danced together with her cheek pressed into his chest until the band played a faster song again. She stayed there for a moment longer than necessary, reluctant to have their connection broken. Heat rose to her cheeks.

"I'd better check on how the cleanup is going."

He nodded and released her hands. "I'll check on Alex."

∽

Her staff had things under control and she was on her way back to Jake when Gretchen stopped her outside the dance tent.

"Hey, I'm glad I found you."

"What's going on?" Maggie's eyes darted to the dance tent. She badly wanted to get back to Jake. Between the party going well, the wine and after dinner drinks she'd had, and the slow dancing with Jake, she was flushed and feeling good about things.

Gretchen however, didn't look so happy.

Maggie narrowed her eyes. "What?"

Her friend sighed. "I'm sorry, but I just got a phone call from my real estate agent friend who has the listing for the Sorensen farm."

"He called you on the weekend?"

"Yeah. Apparently there's been some interest in the property." She took a deep breath. "I'm sorry Maggie, but they've got an offer."

Maggie's stomach dropped. "What does that mean? Will they take it? How much is it for?"

"I don't know any of the details. My friend said the owner is willing to wait for twenty-four hours before he accepts the existing offer if you'd like to put in one of your own."

"So should I do it?" Maggie asked slowly. She wasn't used to feeling so indecisive. Buying the café had been an easy decision since she had worked there for a few years first. But this was an idea that had come to her in the last week and meant taking a huge risk. Uncertainty swirled around her.

"Look, you don't have to decide now." Gretchen patted her arm. "Think about it overnight and get back to me by noon tomorrow. If you decide to put in an offer, we can develop a competitive plan."

Maggie pursed her lips. "Thanks, Gretchen. I appreciate your help with this."

"No problem. What good is it to have a real estate agent for a friend if you can't count on them for big purchases like this?" Gretchen grinned. "Now get in there. I saw you dancing with Jake earlier, pressed up against him like he was a second skin."

Maggie blushed. "It wasn't like that," she protested.

"Uh-huh. You were having the time of your life. Go, have fun. And if something happens between you and him, let it happen! You've got to get out in the dating world."

"Gretchen!" Maggie said, but her friend just waved and walked away.

She had enjoyed Jake's touch, but what did that mean? He'd always been a ladies' man in the past and she was more of a serious relationship kind of girl. Would it even work between them? She pictured them slow dancing together again and entered the tent with rosy cheeks.

"Hey." He stood when he saw her. "Is everything okay? You look a little flushed."

"Yes. No." She paused. "Everything is okay with the catering job, but not so much with the farm property we looked at." She remembered what he thought about the Sorensen property. "Not that you care."

"Maggie. You know that's not true."

She felt him search her face.

"I care about you, and I care about things that are important to you." He pulled her against his chest.

She felt tears come to her eyes as she relaxed and snuggled close to him. It was nice to have someone else taking care of her for a change. She turned her face upward to look at him. "But you don't think I should buy the farm property?"

He sighed. "I don't know what to tell you. It's risky and will take a lot of work. Only you can make that decision."

She closed her eyes and buried her face in his chest. "I know," she murmured.

They stood like that for a minute. A slow song came on and they swayed together gently in place. She felt safe and loved, something she hadn't experienced since Brian's death. She looked up and scanned his face. He wore a dreamy expression and his eyes locked with hers. Her heart beat faster. Was this it? Was something going to happen between them? She hadn't finished weighing the pros and cons of a relationship with her brother-in-law. Before she could spiral deeper into doubt, he bent his head and brushed his lips against hers.

She leaned in closer and deepened the kiss. Everything around them seemed to disappear and it was as though it was only the two of them, swaying to the music in their own winter wonderland.

Then the music changed to a fast song and they broke apart reluctantly. Slowly, the rest of the people in the tent came into focus.

Had people seen them kissing? A jolt hit her. Alex. Had Alex seen them together? She didn't know how he would react to seeing his mom and uncle kissing. Still holding Jake's hand, she spun around to where she'd last seen her son. He was in the corner with his friend, engrossed in playing on a tablet.

"Are you okay?" Jake asked.

"Yeah, I was checking on Alex. I don't think he saw us."

He pulled her close again, sending her pulse racing.

"Are you worried about what he'll think if we're together?"

"Yes." She looked at him closer. "Is that what's happening? Are we together?"

He brushed the side of her cheek with the pad of his thumb, sending a tingling sensation throughout her body. "I'd like to be. How do you feel about it?"

She smiled. She hadn't felt this happy in ages. "Good. I'd like to see where this goes." She frowned. "But I don't know how Alex will react."

"Well, I think you're about to find out." He pointed behind her.

"What?" She whipped around and found Alex standing two feet away, looking between her and his uncle.

"What's going on?" he asked.

Jake cleared his throat. "I'd like to ask your mother out on a date. Would that be okay with you?"

A smile spread across Alex's face. "Uh-huh." He tugged on Maggie's hand. "Mom, say yes!"

She bent down and hugged him tightly. "Thanks, buddy."

"Can I go back and play with Andy some more?"

"Yes." She patted him on the back. "Have fun, honey."

When he left she looked at Jake, raising her eyebrows. "Well, that was easy."

He laughed. "I wasn't sure how he'd feel, but I hoped he'd be happy to have us together. He mentioned a few times that you were lonely and didn't go out much."

Her face burned. "I am not lonely."

He wrapped his arm around her waist and kissed the top of her head. "I didn't say you were."

At the front of the room, one of Garrett's groomsmen tapped on the microphone. "Alright, ladies and gentleman, Dahlia and Garrett are about to toss the bouquet and garter."

Dahlia beamed and held the flowers high in the air above her. The crowd cheered.

"Alright, all the single ladies—gather over here." She pointed to a space in front of her.

Maggie hung back next to Jake.

"Mags! Get over here!" Gretchen grabbed her hand and pulled her into the teeming mass of women.

"Oh, fine." Maggie positioned herself at the edge of the crowd, not intending to try for the bouquet. They watched as Dahlia said, "Ready?" She winked at Maggie and tossed the bouquet.

Maggie kept her arms down as the other women around her, including Gretchen, clamored to catch the flowers. The beautiful bouquet flew high up over the crowd and sailed straight into Maggie's forehead. She instinctively held out her hands to catch it before it could hit the floor. She stared at it, unsure of how she felt.

"Congrats, Maggie." Gretchen clapped her on the back, smiling.

Maggie looked up at Dahlia, who grinned at her and gave her a thumbs-up. Maggie's jaw dropped. Dahlia had thrown it her way on purpose!

"And now for the garter toss." The DJ who'd taken over from the band later in the evening began playing a catchy tune. Dahlia sat on a chair and pulled the skirt of her wedding dress up to her knee. Garrett leaned down and winked at the men gathered near them and then removed the beaded garter from his wife's leg. He twirled it around on one finger and then flung it into the crowd. The crowd cheered and the victor held it in the air.

Next to Maggie, Gretchen blushed. Her boyfriend, Parker, was smiling at her from across the room, showing her the garter he'd caught.

Maggie slugged her in the arm. "Looks like I'm not the only one in the hot seat."

Gretchen mock glared at her, but a smile slipped between the cracks. "I'm going to go find Parker. If I don't see you later tonight, I'll see you when we get together later this week, okay?"

"Okay. See you." Maggie scanned the crowd, searching for Jake.

Everyone had started to gather for the cake cutting, making it difficult to find him. She put the bouquet down on the chair where she'd stashed her purse and walked over to the cake as well. She watched as the newly married couple fed each other cake and then kissed.

Could she find happiness like that again? Her kiss with Jake had shown her that she could find it in the short term, but only time would tell if they were meant to be. She shot a glance at the bouquet on the chair and a smile formed on her lips. The bouquet toss was supposed to predict who would be married next. She doubted that it would be her, but you never knew. She wanted to hope for the best.

After the cake, she found Jake eating dessert with Alex.

"It's getting late. I need to get Alex to bed." She smiled at her son and then looked at Jake. Their eyes met and her skin rippled with goose bumps. She breathed in sharply at the familiar sensation. "Call me in an hour?"

He nodded and her stomach flip-flopped.

14

*M*aggie couldn't get Alex into bed fast enough. Luckily, he was so tired from the day's activities that he fell asleep as soon as his head hit the pillow.

She sat on the couch and picked up a magazine. The words swam in front of her eyes. All she could think about was Jake. His touch, his kiss. Things had come together between them so quickly that evening, it seemed like a dream.

The phone rang and she lunged for it. "Hello," she said breathlessly.

"Hi, Maggie." Her name rolled off his tongue with so much familiarity, sending shivers down her spine.

There was a brief moment of quiet.

"So is this where I get to officially ask you out on a date?"

She nodded, although she knew he couldn't see her. "It is."

"What do you think about dinner tomorrow? We could go somewhere in Haven Shores? Are your parents back to watch Alex?"

"No, they're still on their big adventure. And the babysitter is out of town this week."

Her earlier excitement deflated. Dating with kids was harder than she'd expected.

"How about I come there and we do pizza and a movie with Alex? It seems fitting since he kind of brought us together. We can share a bottle of wine afterward."

Happiness flooded over her. This was what she'd dreamed about—to have someone in her life that cared about both her and Alex.

"That sounds great. I'll pick out a movie to watch."

"I'll see you around six tomorrow night. Bye, Maggie." Her heart beat faster when he said her name.

"See you tomorrow."

He hung up and she stared at the phone. Were things moving too fast between them? Did she even remember how to date? She stared at the wall. She was being silly. It had been so long since she'd been on a date, she'd forgotten how things worked. Dinner and a movie were pretty basic. She could handle it, right?

~

The next evening, Jake showed up at Maggie's apartment door, freshly shaven and wearing a crisply ironed shirt. He carried a pepperoni pizza that he'd picked up on the way over. He was so nervous, he wasn't sure he'd be able to eat.

He was about to knock on the door when it opened suddenly.

"Hi," Maggie said brightly. "Alex is waiting in the living room for you."

He walked past her as she shut the door, kissing her on the head. She blushed and took the pizza into the kitchen.

"I'll get some plates," she called over her shoulder.

He grinned. He liked seeing how she reacted to his kiss.

"Hey, Alex." He settled down next to his nephew on the couch. "What are we watching tonight?"

"Mom said something called Indiana Jones? She said it's one of her favorite movies and that I'm finally old enough to watch it." He looked disappointed. "I wanted to watch a cartoon."

Jake ruffled his hair and smiled. He and Maggie had similar taste in movies apparently. "Seriously? That's awesome. You'll love Indiana Jones. He goes on so many adventures."

"I guess." The boy pushed himself further into the couch cushions.

Maggie appeared in the living room with the pizza box and a stack of plates. "Here you go." She handed them each a plate with pizza on it.

"Thanks," they mumbled as they devoured the pizza.

Maggie smiled. "How do you guys eat so fast? I'd be sick if I did that."

They shrugged and continued munching. Maggie sat down about a foot away from Jake at the other end of the sofa. He moved a little closer to the middle of the couch. No snuggling for them during the movie. This was what dating with kids was like.

She clicked play and the movie came on. For being so negative about the movie in the beginning, Alex watched it with rapt attention, cringing and covering his eyes at the scary parts. When the movie ended, he looked disappointed.

"Okay, buddy, bedtime for you." Maggie pointed at the hallway.

"Do I have to? Can't I stay up a little longer?"

She shook her head. "Sorry. It's a school night. I already let you stay up a little past bedtime."

"Fine." Alex pouted and trudged down the hall.

"I'll come tuck you in in about ten minutes," she called to him. "I'll grab the wine," she told Jake.

He nodded. "I'll help."

He followed her into the kitchen, putting his arm around her waist to pull her into his arms. She melted into him for a moment before glancing toward Alex's room.

"Jake," she protested. "What if Alex sees us?"

"He's brushing his teeth," he said, but kissed her quickly and released her.

She removed the Pinot Grigio from the refrigerator and set it on the counter. He remembered where the wine glasses were in the top cupboard from a previous visit and selected two, then corked the wine and poured them each a glass.

"I'm going to go tuck Alex in, okay?" Maggie disappeared into the hallway.

Jake brought the wine glasses into the living room and settled on the couch while she checked on Alex. It felt right to be there, like he was truly a part of their family.

She reappeared fifteen minutes later. "He's out. It usually takes him longer to fall asleep, but it's a bit later than his usual bedtime."

He patted the seat next to him. This time, she settled in a little closer than when they were watching the movie earlier. She reached forward for her wine glass and then leaned back.

"Ahh. I'm so glad this week is over. I loved catering Dahlia's rehearsal dinner and wedding, but I'll be glad when life is back to normal."

"Well, you did a wonderful job on them. If the glowing

comments I heard from the other guests were any indication, I'd say you have a future career as a caterer." He slid his arm over the back of the couch. "What did you decide about the farm property?"

She set the base of her wine glass on her leg. "They received another offer yesterday. Gretchen told me last night." She took a big sip of wine. "I couldn't pull together my offer quick enough to compete with them, so I guess that's that."

"I'm sorry. I know it meant a lot to you." He rested his fingers on her shoulder and she moved in closer to him.

"You know, real estate offers sometimes fall through. Maybe you should put a backup offer on the property."

"Do you think?"

He felt her search his face. "I do." He'd been unsure about the property before, but after thinking about it for a while and knowing how important it was to her, he'd determined it was a good idea.

"Maybe I'll do that." She brightened. "I'll call Gretchen in the morning."

She lay against him, sipping her wine, lost in thought.

He looked at her and marveled at how he had a chance with her. His brother may not have intended for this to happen when he'd asked Jake to look after her if something happened to him, but he was pretty sure he'd approve. Not that he could ever let Maggie know about his promise to Brian.

He stroked her hair and relished their brief time alone together.

15

*M*aggie woke the next morning feeling happier than she had in a long time. She still had a few minutes until she needed to wake up Alex for school, so she made a pot of coffee and sat at the kitchen table to drink her first cup of the day. It may be weird to be dating her brother-in-law, but it felt right. Then she glanced at the calendar, and ice slammed into her. It was December eighteenth. This would have been her eleventh wedding anniversary. She leaned back in her chair.

How had she forgotten her wedding anniversary? She'd been busy with Dahlia's wedding, the catering business and shopping for Christmas presents, but she'd never forgotten her anniversary before. She walked into the living room and picked up the picture of Brian and her on their wedding day. As usual, he smiled at her from inside the frame. Her eyes teared up. He'd been gone for five years. Was she forgetting him? She didn't want to forget him. Dating Jake had seemed so natural, but was it the right thing to do?

She heard Alex moving around and set the picture back on the table.

"What's going on, Mom? Why are you crying?"

She swiped at her tears. "It's nothing, honey. I was just thinking about your dad. We were married eleven years ago today."

"Oh," he said. "Are you okay?"

She hugged him. "Yeah, I'm okay. I just miss him sometimes."

"Me too. Well, I miss what I think it would be like to have him around." He was quiet for a moment. "But it's been nice to have Jake around. It's almost like having Dad here."

She could only nod her head for fear of breaking out in a fresh round of tears.

"Why don't you go get ready for school? I laid your clothes out in the bathroom. How about I make pancakes today for breakfast?"

"Cool, pancakes!" He ran off down the hall.

As soon as he was out of sight, she allowed the tears to fall freely for a minute before drying her eyes and putting on a brave face for her son. She took him to school after he finished his pancakes and then went to work, intent on not thinking about her anniversary again until that night.

However, when she was alone in her office at the café, memories of Brian kept flashing into her head. She tried to focus on the next week's staffing schedule, but it was too boring to compete with her obsessive brain. She clicked on the real estate website she'd looked at before. There had to be something else out there that wouldn't be as expensive as the Sorensen farm. After all, she didn't need the farmhouse, only the event space.

An abandoned warehouse on the outskirts of town caught her eye. It wasn't as picturesque as the barn, but it could work. Maybe seeing the property would take her mind off of her wedding anniversary. On impulse, she dialed her friend.

"Hey, Gretchen, I have a favor to ask."

"Sure, what's up?"

"I found another property online that might work for the event center. It's that old warehouse out on the highway. Any chance you could show it to me today?"

She held her breath as she listened to Gretchen clicking away on her computer.

"You're in luck. It's got a lockbox, so I don't need to contact the owner first. Let me check my schedule." More clicking. "I've got an opening in an hour. Can you meet me at my office then?"

Maggie looked around her office. Her to-do list was piling up, but she wasn't getting much accomplished there. "Yep, I'll see you then."

She tried to stay on task as much as possible for the next hour, but excitement over the prospective event space kept her from fully focusing. When there were only five minutes to go until their appointment, she couldn't wait any longer. She gathered up her belongings and informed her staff she was going out.

Gretchen drove them to the warehouse. The parking lot and exterior were bleaker than they'd appeared. The area was surrounded with empty lots and lacked charm. It also lacked any exterior scenery, so she'd only be able to have indoor events. Perhaps that was good, because she couldn't go overboard with plans in the startup phase. Besides, maybe the inside would be better.

It wasn't.

The windows were high off the ground and cracked, letting in very little natural light. Dirt coated the floors and walls. An odd smell permeated the building.

"What was this place?" Gretchen wrinkled her nose. "It stinks."

"I don't know. The listing didn't say." Maggie tried to ignore the odor, but Gretchen was right, the inside smelled funky. There was no real comparison to the Sorensen farm. She'd decided not to put in a backup offer on the farm property because of the high cost. Had that been a mistake? Would another comparable property ever come up?

She sighed. "Let's go."

Gretchen nodded and put her arm around her. "Don't worry, something else will come up. We'll find you the right space."

Maggie hoped so. At least touring the warehouse had been a good diversion. She returned to work and tried to stay off the internet. She needed to keep up-to-date on café business if she ever wanted a chance to expand further into catering.

That night, after Alex was in bed, she poured herself a glass of the leftover wine from the night before and allowed her mind to wander back to Brian. She'd been thinking a lot about how she'd felt that morning. It wasn't that she felt guilty about dating Jake. She knew Brian would want her to move on. It was just that she didn't want to lose her memories of their time together. He'd been a big part of her life and she wanted to keep his memory alive. She looked down the hall at Alex's closed bedroom door and smiled. Brian would always be alive through his son. She lay back on the couch. Every year since Brian's death, their anniversary date stung, but every year it affected her less and less. Life moved on, as it should.

The phone rang. *I hope that's not Jake*, she thought.

It wasn't Jake, but even worse, it was her mother-in-law. She loved her mother-in-law, but she wasn't sure how she was going to get through a conversation with her without breaking down.

"Hi, Maggie," Barbara said.

"Hi." Maggie sat up, bringing her knees to her chest.

"I was thinking of Brian today and remembering how lovely your wedding was, so I thought I'd call you. I hope you don't mind." She sounded teary.

"Thanks for thinking of me." Maggie choked back her own tears. A thought struck her. What would Barbara say if she knew that Maggie and her son were dating? Would she think it odd? Had Jake already told her? She didn't want to ask.

"I've been thinking about Brian a lot lately too. I miss him." She had to reach for the Kleenex box.

"Us too." Barbara was quiet for a moment. "Let's talk about something happier. Are you and Alex still coming down to Portland after Christmas?"

"Yes, we're still planning on it. Probably around the twenty-ninth. Fingers crossed nothing goes wrong at the café before then. Alex is looking forward to seeing you."

"And how's Jake doing? He's sounded in good spirits when I've talked with him on the phone. I have to say I'm surprised that he decided to settle in Candle Beach."

"You and me both," Maggie said. It probably had something to do with her, but she wasn't going to tell Barbara that. "He seems to be enjoying it here. I think he likes the small-town atmosphere after moving around so much."

"You're probably right. And having you and Alex around is good for him. I get the feeling he didn't have much time for close relationships when he was in the service. It's a hard life."

"Yes. It is." Maggie knew that all too well. Being a child-less Army wife hadn't made making friends easy. While she'd loved Brian, she hadn't loved the loneliness of being away from all her family and friends. She'd never considered it from the soldier's perspective. It must have been a lonely life for Jake too. No wonder he'd quickly become attached to small-town living.

"Maggie?" Barbara's voice sounded hesitant.

"Yeah?"

"You know it's okay to move on, right? Brian would have wanted you to be happy and remarry. Not only for you, but for Alex."

Maggie had to cover the phone to blow her nose. "I know," she said shakily.

"I'm sorry, honey, I didn't mean to upset you. I just wanted to remind you it was okay to live again. I'll let you go. Maybe we can talk in a few days?"

"Don't worry about it. I'm fine. Thanks. I'll talk to you later."

She hung up. Her mother-in-law was right. She knew it was okay to move on, but was she ready? And did Barbara know she'd started a relationship with Jake? This was all so confusing, but she knew she'd have to figure out soon what she wanted.

~

After the stress of her wedding anniversary and losing out on the Sorensen farm, Maggie needed to relax a little. A girls' night was exactly what she needed.

She waved at Charlotte and Gretchen, who were already seated in a booth at Off the Vine, the town's wine bar. She scooted onto the seat next to Charlotte and reached for the menu. "I'm starving. Did you guys already order?"

"Not yet." Charlotte shoved the menu at her. "We're

thinking about the stuffed mushroom caps and the fig and chèvre flatbread to start."

"Ooh, sounds yummy." She studied the menu. "How about the pita and hummus platter too?"

They nodded. The waitress came over and they placed their food and drink orders.

"Dahlia's missing out," Gretchen joked.

"Yeah, poor girl. She's missing out on the beautiful gray weather we're having and is stuck in sunny Jamaica." Maggie sipped her water and made a face at the wintry weather outside the window.

"I want to honeymoon somewhere tropical." Gretchen's face took on a dreamy expression.

"You'll need to get engaged first." Charlotte winked at her.

"True." Gretchen blushed and peeked at them over her water glass. "Parker and I have been talking about marriage lately."

"Wow, that's crazy. First Dahlia, now you." Maggie shook her head.

"I'm not getting married anytime soon. We're going to take it slow and figure out what we want out of life," Gretchen said hastily. "We just wanted to check in with how we were feeling about our long-term relationship goals." She turned to Maggie. "What about you and Jake? You looked like you were getting pretty cozy at Dahlia's wedding.

It was her turn to blush. "We've decided to try things out between us." She shrugged. "I don't know if it will work or not."

"Well, I'm glad you're giving him a chance." Gretchen smiled at her. "He's a good guy—and he's crazy about you."

"I think he's a good guy too." An image of Jake playing with Alex flashed into her head. He really would be a good father. Then she stopped herself. What was she thinking? They'd only been dating for a few days and she was already imagining herself married to him? She hastily changed the subject.

"So, Charlotte, how are sales at Whimsical Delights? I refer customers there all the time to get unique souvenirs from Candle Beach."

"Thanks." Charlotte patted her mouth with her napkin. "Things are going better than I expected. I thought the winter season would be really slow, but sales have been steady."

"That's great." Maggie sipped her drink. "Gretchen, are you and Parker going to start your real estate business soon?"

"Yes, we're working on what we want the company to look like and where we want to focus our sales efforts. It should be up and running by early spring." She beamed. "I'm so excited! I'm finally going to be branching out on my own."

It was good to see her friends so happy and fulfilled, but it reminded Maggie that there was still so much she wanted to do. The café was still important to her, of course, but she was ready for a new challenge. The farm property may have already sold, but if something else came up, she knew she needed to be prepared.

"You okay?" Gretchen asked, a concerned look on her face.

Maggie focused on her friend. "Yeah, sorry, I was just thinking about the event space I wanted to purchase."

"Sorry the farm sold. It would have been perfect." Gretchen frowned. "I'm keeping an eye out for other properties that will work though, okay?"

"Thanks." It didn't hurt to keep her options open.

"Hey, did you guys hear about the bank robbery in Haven Shores today? I was down there getting some supplies for my shop and there were police cars all over near the State Street bank." Charlotte sipped her drink.

"Yeah, one of my clients mentioned it," said Gretchen. "Apparently one of the bank robbers shot at the police. One police officer was hit in the leg and had to go to the hospital." She shook her head. "The robbers got away. Scary."

Maggie's face blanched and chills shot up her spine. It hadn't occurred to her that Jake's job could be dangerous. It should have, but with everything else going on in her life, it was one thing she hadn't obsessed over. Now, the danger he could face was crystal clear. As a military wife, she'd always had it in mind that something bad could happen to her husband. After having her worst nightmares come true with Brian's death in a war zone, could she handle worrying about Jake on a daily basis?

"Okay, now what's wrong?" Gretchen peered into her face. "I swear, I've never seen you so distracted. Is this what dating does to you?"

"No," Maggie said, more sharply than she'd intended. Charlotte stared at her with wide eyes.

She sighed. "Sorry guys. Until you mentioned that robbery, I didn't even think about how dangerous Jake's job is."

Charlotte's face fell. "I'm so sorry, I didn't think first before I mentioned it." She smacked her forehead with her palm. "I knew Jake had been hired by the police department here. I shouldn't have said anything." She looked at Maggie anxiously. "Are you okay?"

Maggie put her arm around Charlotte. "It's not your fault. Before Brian died, I tried not to let it get to me that his job could be dangerous. I never watched the news while he was in the

Middle East so it wouldn't make me crazy with worry. And then my fears came true anyways." Tears streamed down her face.

Charlotte pulled her close and Gretchen handed her a tissue.

"Oh, Maggie. It's okay. Jake's a member of the Candle Beach Police department. I don't think dangerous things ever happen here, so you don't need to worry." Charlotte squeezed her shoulder as Maggie dried her tears.

She looked around the wine bar. Nobody appeared to be watching her outburst. She gulped her drink. "So you think I'm silly to worry?"

"No, not silly. But, I don't think you need to let it affect your relationship." Charlotte smiled at her reassuringly.

Maggie slumped down in her seat. "But how do I forget that he could be in danger every time he goes to work?"

Gretchen shrugged. "You can't. But if you want a relationship with Jake to work, you have to accept him, job and all."

"I don't know if I can do that." Maggie was quiet for a moment.

"Let's talk about something more cheerful," Charlotte said. "Has anyone seen that huge house going up on Alder street?"

~

The next night, Jake showed up at Maggie's apartment with a bouquet of flowers for her.

"Thanks, they're beautiful." She sniffed the roses and disappeared inside her apartment, presumably to put them in a vase.

Jake waited outside for her, excited to go on their first

real date. Her parents had invited Alex to spend the night with them, leaving her free for a dinner alone.

She returned to the door and smiled brightly at him. She wore an emerald-green sweater over a gray skirt that emphasized her curves. He wondered again how he'd been so lucky to take her out on a date.

"How does Chinese sound? There's a place called Lu's down the street from the B&B." The smells coming from the Chinese restaurant tantalized him every time he walked past.

"Sounds good. I love Lu's." Maggie's skirt swung with every step she took.

He held his arm out to her and she looped her arm through his.

"I feel so free. I hate the early morning shifts, but it sure is nice to have the evening off."

The evening was chilly but clear, and they walked the half mile to Main Street. Lu's was decked out in gaudy Christmas lights, but he had to admit the overall effect of the town's decorating efforts was charming. He grabbed Maggie's hand and pulled her inside the restaurant. It smelled even better inside than outside. The restaurant featured red—lots of it. Gold cats and other knickknacks smiled down on him from a ledge near the cash register.

"Maggie." An Asian man in his sixties beamed at her. "Who's this with you?"

She looked at Jake with uncertainty.

"This is Jake, my...uh...boyfriend. Jake, this is Mr. Lu, the owner."

"Ah, I'm glad to meet you." He shook Jake's hand.

"Good to meet you too."

Mr. Lu showed them to a small booth in the back of the

restaurant. Maggie slid in on the far side and Jake took the seat across from her.

"So what's good here?" He ran his finger down each listing on the extensive menu.

"Almost everything. I'm not a fan of the moo shu pork, but I've never really liked it anywhere."

"How about getting a family-style meal? That way we get a good sampling. I'd love to find a good Chinese place up here."

"Sounds good." Maggie flagged down Mr. Lu and they ordered.

After ordering, they sat at the table staring at each other. Jake's heart pounded. What if they had nothing to say to each other now that they were alone?

He searched for a topic, landing on something that was popular at work. "So did you hear about that bank robbery in Haven Shores yesterday? The station's been abuzz about it all day. Apparently those bandits have been hitting banks up and down the coast." He peered at Maggie, who appeared lost in thought. He waved his hand in front of her face. "Hello?"

Her eyes finally met his. "Sorry. Yes, I did hear about the bank robbery." She didn't say anything else, and he fought to think of another topic of conversation.

"How's Alex?"

Her face brightened and she told him all about Alex's latest Lego creation. He loved seeing her face light up when she spoke of her son.

Then she stopped, looking embarrassed. "Sorry. I'm boring you, aren't I? I've been talking about Alex too much. We can talk about something else if you'd like. It's been so long since I was out on a real date, I've forgotten how to have an adult conversation."

He smiled. "No, it's fine. I like hearing what he's up to. Now that I've started my job, I don't get to hang out with my little buddy as much as I'd like."

Their food came and they dug in.

"Mmm. This is really good." Jake shoveled fried rice into his mouth.

"Told you so." Maggie hummed softly as she picked up chow mein with her chopsticks, eating faster than was ladylike.

He loved how comfortable she was with him. He'd been out on some dates where his companion only ate a few forkfuls of salad and then claimed they were full. Maggie wasn't like that. Everything about her spoke of her honesty.

After dinner, they walked down to the Marina Park.

"Hard to believe this was full of tents for Dahlia's wedding only a week ago." Maggie grabbed his hand and led him to the swings. "This is one of my favorite places in Candle Beach. I've been coming here to swing since I was a baby. I love how when you swing high, you can see the ocean."

They swung companionably for a few minutes until Maggie jumped off and beckoned for him to walk with her. "C'mon. I'll show you another of my favorite places."

She led him over to a bench on a hillside overlooking the water. There weren't many other people out on this cold winter evening and all of the benches lining the hillside were empty.

They sat down and she snuggled up to him. He smiled and wrapped his arm around her shoulders. "It's beautiful here. I see why you love it so much."

She nodded and tucked her head against his chest.

Below them, the waves crashed upon the beach, their frothy tips illuminated by the moon. The wind blew slightly, but their heavy winter coats protected them from the brunt of it. He kissed the top of her head and watched as she smiled.

She turned her head up to look into his eyes.

He leaned down and kissed her lightly. As she responded to his touch, he deepened the kiss and she wrapped her arms around his neck. He positioned his hands around her waist.

"I feel like I'm kissing a marshmallow," he said. "This coat must be eight inches thick."

She grinned and smacked him on the chest. "Thanks a lot."

She leaned back on the bench and they stared out at the water together. He began to softly sing an old song that his father used to sing about a girl named Maggie. She bolted upright and stared at him like a deer caught in the headlights.

"What's wrong?" He could hear the terror in his voice.

She averted her eyes. "It's nothing."

She walked away and he jogged to catch up with her. He placed his hand on her shoulder to stop her. "What is it?"

She turned and his eyes widened. Tears were falling down her face. He pulled her close, but her arms hung limply by her side.

"Maggie. Tell me."

"Brian used to sing me that song. It was kind of our thing."

He closed his eyes. He'd really stepped in this one. "I didn't know. It's something Dad used to sing to us when we were little kids."

"It's okay." Her eyes were red from crying. "Things like this are bound to come up, right?" A haunted expression clouded her face. "You sounded so much like him though."

He hugged her and this time she reciprocated his touch.

"I should get home," she whispered. "I have to be at the café at five tomorrow morning."

"Okay."

They walked hand in hand back to her apartment. Something about their connection had broken.

He kissed her goodnight and she closed the door. He swiveled with his hands in his pockets. What had happened? The evening had been going well and then a simple song had derailed everything. Was Maggie over his brother? He never wanted to take Brian's place in Maggie and Alex's life, but he did want to forge his own place in their family. Would he ever have the chance to do that?

~

Maggie closed the door on Jake and slid to the floor. He must think she was crazy after she broke down from a simple song. He'd been very apologetic after she panicked, but he'd obviously been upset by her behavior.

She knew she'd overreacted, but the incident also made her worried that she wasn't ready to date again. But she really, really liked Jake and he cared about her and Alex. It had been five years since Brian's death. She needed to put herself out there and allow herself to love again. But with his dangerous job, could she do that?

------

16

*T*he next day, Maggie unlocked the front door of the café early in the morning. She hesitated outside, allowing herself to see the town in its pre-dawn state.

The lampposts were draped with strings of white lights and the store owners had decked out their windows with Christmas displays and colored lights. The air was crisp, but a layer of fog hung over Main Street. She loved this town and knew she was lucky to live there. Moving with the military, she and Brian had often lived in places that weren't near the water and she felt like a little piece of her soul died with every day spent away from the magnificent ocean. She breathed in more of the salty air and opened the door, glancing ruefully at the Help Wanted sign on the front window.

Bernadette had left two weeks ago, and Maggie had even put an ad in the Haven Shores newspaper for a new pastry chef, but there hadn't been any applicants. She had been doing all the baking, with some help from a few of her employees. The Bluebonnet Café had a history of offering whole pies for sale every Christmas, but she'd made the decision not to do so this year. There just wasn't enough time for her to make the quantity of pies they'd need for the community. She knew there would be some frustration from her customers, but there was nothing she could do about it.

She relocked the door behind her and flipped on lights as she walked back to her office. The morning crew would be there by six, but she liked to have a few minutes alone to get her day organized before everyone arrived and chaos reigned.

She pored over the bills and lost track of time. When Velma barged into her office without knocking, she looked up in annoyance. "Good morning," she said.

"It's not a good morning," Velma replied. "The milk and egg delivery hasn't arrived yet and we're almost out. Things like this didn't happen when Gus owned the place."

Maggie gritted her teeth. She couldn't control the milkman's delivery schedule, even if Velma seemed to think she could. "I'll call the dairy and find out what's going on. Thanks for letting me know." She smiled at her employee, determined to kill her with kindness.

Velma stared at her with suspicion. "Hmph. Bill at the dairy probably stopped for a coffee break. He's never here on time."

Maggie had never know the milkman to be late except when there were extenuating circumstances, so she said pleasantly, "I'll give him a call." She looked pointedly at the door and Velma huffed her way out.

She found the dairy's number and called. "Hey Bill, sorry to bother you, but we haven't received our order this morning."

"Oh, I meant to call you, but things got hectic here. We had a calf born last night that needed medical attention and

I had to call the vet. I'll be out there in about thirty minutes. I'm sorry about the inconvenience. I'll throw in a couple gallons of ice cream too for free."

She grinned. This was another thing she loved about small town life. Her local suppliers were real people and they cared about each other.

"No problem. We'll make do until then. I hope the calf is okay."

"Yup, she'll be fine. Thanks Maggie. See you soon." He hung up.

Maggie went out to the kitchen to let the staff know the status of the dairy order. There was some grumbling from Velma, but she knew they'd figure things out until the order arrived.

Customers were lining up already at the hostess desk. Her hostess wasn't scheduled until eight o'clock, so she filled in until she arrived. Then she disappeared back into her office to tackle the remaining accounting tasks.

A call came in from her mother's number. "I oke a ooth."

"What?" Maggie stared at the phone. It sounded like her mom, but she couldn't understand her.

"I oke a ooth. Octor Han is going to fit me in today at one, but I can't watch Alex this afternoon."

"You have to go to the dentist this afternoon because you broke a tooth and you can't watch Alex." Maggie sighed inwardly. Having Alex home on Winter Break made every-thing more complicated. Where was she going to find a babysitter on such short notice? Was Stacey available?

"I'll pick him up at a quarter to one, okay?"

Her mother made an affirmative noise.

Maggie found the contact info for Stacey and called her. Hopefully she was back in town by now.

Surprisingly, she was in luck.

"Sure, I'd be happy to babysit Alex. I'll pick him up at a quarter to one from your mom's house. We can go to the park or something."

Maggie sighed in relief. "Thanks Stacey. I really appreciate this. I know it was short notice."

"No problem. I feel bad that I couldn't help you out when I was sick. I'll see you later."

Phew. Two problems solved already and it wasn't even noon yet. She hadn't even had time to worry about Jake's job.

She worked on paperwork for the rest of the day until it was almost time for her to get off at two o'clock.

"We've got forty orders for Christmas pies. Twenty-five mincemeat and fifteen apple," Velma barked at her after barging into her office for the second time that day.

Maggie's jaw dropped. "What do you mean, orders for pies?"

"You hadn't put up a sign yet for pie orders, so I had to make one. People have been waiting to order. You've really got to get things more organized. Why, we could have lost business from not having the sign up."

In carefully measured tones, Maggie said, "The reason there was no sign up for pies was because we don't have the staff to make them. After Bernadette left, we've been short a baker."

"Well, you'd better hire someone then, because people will want their pies." She huffed then spun on her heels and out the door.

Maggie called after her, "Please take the sign down. We can't fill any more orders." There was no response to acknowledge Velma had heard her directive.

Maggie shut her door and locked it. She couldn't take having Velma come in again anytime soon. How the heck was she going to make forty pies? She needed a new pastry chef ASAP.

Someone knocked timidly at her door. "Maggie? You in there?"

She sighed and unlocked the door. Lily stood in front of her.

"There's someone here who wants to apply for the baking job."

Maggie stared upwards. Her guardian angel must be watching over her today.

Out in the lobby, a woman stood in front of the menu, twisting her fingers. She had long, straight, dark hair and a heart-shaped face. She appeared to be in her mid-twenties. Maggie's enthusiasm dropped a notch. How much baking experience could she possibly have?

Maggie approached her and stuck out her hand. "Hi, I'm Maggie. I'm the owner of the Bluebonnet Café."

The woman shook her hand. "I'm Angel. I saw you were looking for a baker?" She pointed to the sign in the window.

"Yes, we are." Maggie leaned against the edge of the pastry case. "Are you interested in the job?"

The woman nodded.

"Great!" Maggie said brightly. "Let's go find a seat and we can discuss the position."

When they were seated at a two-seater table in the back of the restaurant, she looked at Angel. The younger woman perched on the edge of her seat.

"So what kind of baking experience do you have?"

"I attended pastry school in Southern California and worked at a bakery in Los Angeles for three years."

Maggie let out the breath she'd been holding. She'd hoped her new applicant would have real experience, but this was better than she'd expected. Angel really was like an angel sent from above.

"That's great to hear." She told her a little about the job. "Are you interested? It would be a lot of early mornings."

Angel grinned, showing two rows of perfectly straight teeth. "I'm used to early mornings."

"Then you're hired." Maggie smiled at her newest employee. "When can you start?" She knew she should have done a background check on Angel, but she had an immediate need for a baker and she had a gut feeling that the new girl would work out.

"Does tomorrow work? I just got to town and I need to find a place to live."

"Tomorrow's fine. Try the Beehive B&B. My boyfriend has been staying there and he loves it." A little thrill shot through her upon calling Jake her boyfriend.

"Thanks for the recommendation. I'll check it out. What time do I start tomorrow?"

Maggie thought about the forty pies she needed to bake in the next couple of days. "Five? Is that too early on your first day?"

"No problem. I'll be there. Thanks for giving me a chance." They shook hands and Angel left the room, with more bounce in her step than when Maggie first saw her.

She checked in on the kitchen staff, and finding everything going according to plan, she left to go get Alex before any other issues could break loose.

17

The next day, Maggie returned to the Bluebonnet Café through the back alley door after going home for lunch. Instead of the normal cacophony of pots and pans and sizzling grills, the kitchen was silent. She pushed open the door to the front lobby area, which was buzzing with chatter and a tense energy. Her staff intermixed with customers as they pressed their noses to the glass windows and door. The sound of police sirens filled the air out on Main Street. She'd heard the sirens when she drove up and parked in the back, but she hadn't expected to see a commotion like this out front.

"What's going on?" she asked one of her waitresses.

The woman blushed all the way to the roots of her bleached blonde hair. "Sorry, Maggie, but there was a robbery at the bank. We all wanted to see what was happening." She pointed. "See—every police car in town is there. I think they cornered the robber over near Donut Daze."

Sure enough, the three Candle Beach police cars were circled around the donut shop. She could just make out a man standing opposite the cars.

A loud crack filled the air and the crowd recoiled in horror.

"Oh my goodness," a customer said, lifting her hand to her mouth. Her wrinkled skin had paled under rouged cheeks. "The robber fired at the police officers." Another shot rang out.

Maggie's world stood still and an icy chill numbed her body. Jake was at work today. If every police officer in the city had responded to the call, he would be out there. He could be injured—or worse. At that moment, it hit her how much she cared about him.

She pushed her way through the crowds to look out the window. Her heart beat triple time as she fought to see. First Brian and now Jake. Were her worst fears coming true a second time?

A crowd had gathered down the street about a block away from the donut shop. A police officer had her arms outstretched, urging them not to get any closer. Maggie ran out of the café toward the crowd. She had to know if Jake was hurt. Her eyes darted between the police cars. One officer was talking on his radio, but she didn't see any others. No ambulance had arrived yet. Where was he?

She kept trying to peek around the police officer in charge of crowd control, but wasn't able to see anything. At the edge of the gathering, it looked like she could make it through and get closer. She knew it was dangerous, but she didn't care. She had to know if he was safe.

"You can't go down there." Gretchen's hand held her back. Maggie stared at her friend with wild eyes.

"Jake could be over there. I can't see what's going on."

"It isn't safe, Maggie." Her friend put an arm around her and forced her to wait. Finally, law enforcement called an all-clear and the crowd surged forward. She broke away from Gretchen and tried frantically to locate Jake.

"Maggie," someone called to her.

An arm reached out and caught her. Jake stood before her, dressed in his police uniform, without a scratch on him. She looked over to the crowd and saw they were watching as the suspected bank robber was cuffed and put into a waiting car.

She started sobbing and her legs buckled underneath her. He caught her and pulled her close.

"I thought you were dead," she managed to eke out.

"Oh Maggie, Maggie." He brushed her hair back and wiped a tear away with his thumb. She pressed her face into his cupped hand, memorizing the warmth of his touch and shape of his hand. "I'm so sorry you were scared."

She looked up at him with tears blurring her vision and blubbered, "They said there were shots fired and I knew you'd be here. I was so worried."

Jake smiled and stroked her hair again. "He shot toward the police car, but there wasn't anyone in it. He managed to maim the town square sign though." He pointed to the edge of the grassy lawn.

She stared at the sign. The bullets had hit the wooden sign's edge, splintering off some of the paint. The Chamber of Commerce would need to get it fixed.

She closed her eyes for a moment before gazing at the sign again. "So lucky no one was hurt."

He released her and turned her around to face him. "I've got to get back to the crime scene." He patted her shoulder and looked reassuringly into her eyes. "It's okay. Everyone's fine."

She nodded then watched as he joined his co-workers near one of the police cars. He retrieved a clipboard from the car and scribbled something on it with a pen. He was okay. Everything was okay.

She repeated the mantra to herself, but her eyes kept returning to the mangled sign. It could have been so much worse.

She trudged back to the café. The day's events were exactly what she'd feared. Would she have to live every day wondering if it would be the last time she'd see Jake?

$\sim$

She tossed and turned all night, still unsure of what she should do. The next morning would be Christmas Eve. She lay in bed and stared at the ceiling. She had a rare two days off as the café would be closed on Christmas Day. When she finally woke at seven o'clock, Alex was still in bed. She took an hour to get ready and sat down with her morning coffee and her checklist.

Her parents were hosting a Christmas Eve dinner and Jake would be attending. Her parents had met him before, but this would be the first time they spent a significant amount of time with him. What would they think of him? He was so different from Brian, but wonderful in his own way. And he loved Alex, which was a huge plus in her book.

The thought of dating again, much less being in a serious relationship, made her somewhat queasy. Things with Jake had started out serious even though they hadn't dated long. They both knew this wasn't some fling. As a single parent, she didn't have the luxury of a fling. But it did feel odd to give up some of her independence.

She busied herself preparing the pies and rolls for the evening meal. She rolled out the pastry crust for a berry pie and marveled at how soothing it was to do something so simple. She probably wouldn't have enjoyed the experience so much if she'd had to make the forty-plus pies Velma had committed them to make for customers. Her new hire, Angel, was working out well and had proven to be a talented baker, taking a huge weight off of Maggie's shoulders.

She finished prepping the pies and put them in the oven. Next, she took out the spiral cut ham and mixed up the glaze. Brian had loved ham and she'd made it for every holiday. Did Jake like it too? There was so much she didn't know about him, but she felt oddly close to him just the same.

~

Jake arrived at Maggie's parents' house at six o'clock on the dot. He paused on the porch and took a deep breath before knocking on the door. He'd met her parents before when dropping Alex off, but spending a holiday with them was a whole new ball game.

Maggie opened the door with her hair up in a messy bun and a white apron smudged with something brown. She wore an oven mitt on one hand. "Come in."

He pecked her on the cheek and followed her inside. Her mother Charlene stood at the kitchen sink, drying off her hands. He handed her a bouquet of flowers.

Her face lit up. "Thank you, tulips are my favorite. How did you know?"

"Oh, a little birdie told me so." He winked at Maggie. "What can I do to help?" He looked around the kitchen. With the exception of a pan of fudge that Maggie was cutting into, it was immaculate.

"Nothing. You're our guest. Why don't you head into the

den with Maggie's dad and Alex. We'll be eating in about five minutes.

He nodded. His stomach knotted at the thought of being virtually alone with Maggie's dad, Will. He'd had little interaction with him in the past and Will had been rather reserved.

He entered the den, where Will and Alex were watching a cartoon. Alex's face lit up when he saw his uncle.

"Uncle Jake!" He ran over and hugged him.

Will looked at Jake with approval. "He seems quite taken with you. I'm glad you decided to stay around."

His spirits rose. Maggie's normally taciturn father had complimented him! He realized with a start that he hadn't had to meet the parents of his date since he was in high school. None of his relationships as an adult had been serious enough to warrant meeting the parents or having them meet his. His stomach twisted. Things were moving fast with Maggie, but somehow it felt right. He knew without a doubt that he loved her and wanted to spend the rest of his life with her. But did she feel the same way? She still had the remains of a wall up around her heart and he wasn't sure when she'd let him break through that barrier.

He stuck his fingers in his jacket pocket and ran them along the velvety box in his pocket. He planned to give it to Maggie later that night.

"Dinner!" Charlene called.

They all sat down at the table and Maggie brought in the ham she'd prepared. Her mom followed with numerous sides.

Jake's stomach grumbled. This feast rivaled his mother's cooking.

"This looks delicious, Mrs. Johansen." He dipped his

fork into the pile of mashed potatoes on his plate and put some in his mouth.

"Charlene, please. I think of my mother-in-law when you call me Mrs. Johansen." She grimaced.

"I will." He put more food on his fork.

"Good, right?" Maggie asked. "My mom is famous for her mashed potatoes."

He nodded, his mouth busy eating his third bite of potatoes. "Delicious."

Charlene beamed. "It's nice to have someone else here for the holidays. All my family live out of state and it gets lonely with just the four of us."

"I'm happy to be here."

"How are you liking Candle Beach?" she asked.

"I love it so far. The small-town atmosphere is really a nice change of pace from the big city."

"Maggie tells me you're working for the police department now. How do you like that? I've heard Chief Lee is good to work for."

"So far, so good." He chewed some ham. "I wasn't sure what I'd do after I got out of the Army, but it seems to be a good fit for me."

"And you plan to stay in town?" He felt Will's eyes heavy upon him.

"Yes, sir." He took Maggie's hand. "I've been getting to know your daughter and grandson better. I plan to stay in town for a long time." His eyes met hers and her face filled with joy.

Her father nodded. "Good."

"Ahem." Charlene cleared her throat and looked around the table. She gave her husband the evil eye. "We're happy to have Jake here today. No more interrogations. Now, please pass the green bean casserole."

He looked at her gratefully. He'd forgotten what it was like to be grilled by a girlfriend's parents.

After dinner, he helped clear the table and then pulled Maggie aside. "When do we open presents?"

"What do you mean?"

"Don't you open presents on Christmas Eve?"

She laughed. "No, we save them for Christmas Day. I'd forgotten about the Price family tradition of opening gifts on Christmas Eve." She put her hand on his upper arm and looked around, as if searching for any onlookers. Seeing no one, she kissed him lightly on the lips.

He smiled and wrapped his arms around her waist. He kissed her back and then let go. "I have a present for you, but it can wait until tomorrow."

"I'm looking forward to it." She tapped him on the nose with her index finger.

"So what does your family do after dinner then if you don't open presents?"

"Aha! So you don't know about the board game extravaganza."

He shot her a quizzical look. "No, I must have missed that on the invitation."

"We play Monopoly every year after dinner. We have since I was a little kid. It's our family tradition."

Monopoly? He shrugged. Every family had a different way of doing things, and he intended to be a part of this one for a long time, so he'd better start with the traditions now.

She grabbed his hand and led him into the family room where everyone else had gathered.

~

Maggie watched Jake laugh as he rolled the dice and moved his piece onto Boardwalk.

Her father smiled smugly. "You owe me six hundred dollars."

"Highway robbery." Jake glared at him.

She smiled, her heart filled with joy. She didn't know what she'd been worried about. He fit in with her family, perhaps more so than Brian had. She sobered at the thought of her deceased husband. It still seemed crazy that he'd never get to see his son open Christmas presents. But it had been a long time since he died. She needed to move on, and she knew with all her heart that Jake was the right person.

Alex rolled the dice and landed on one of his grandfather's spaces. "Oh, man."

"Yeah, you and me both, buddy." Jake pulled Alex against him and gave him a hug. "Your grandfather got me too."

Alex relaxed into his chest, his face flushed from the day's excitement.

When the game wrapped up, Maggie packed up to go home. Everyone gathered in the entry hall.

"Thanks for bringing the ham, honey," Charlene said.

"No problem." Maggie hugged her and then her father.

"Thank you for your hospitality." Jake put his arm around Charlene's shoulders and squeezed lightly, then shook Will's hand.

Her parents smiled and waved goodbye to them, kissing Alex as he scooted past.

"Merry Christmas, Grandma and Grandpa!" he shouted from the porch.

Outside of the house, Maggie asked, "Do you want to spend the night at my place?"

He stared at her open-mouthed, and she realized immediately what she'd said.

"Oh. That didn't come out right." Heat crept up her neck. "I meant to sleep on the couch. I thought you might want to see Alex when he wakes up and opens Santa presents."

He smiled at her and took her hand. "I'd love to."

18

*M*aggie tiptoed through the apartment the next morning getting things ready for their traditional Christmas breakfast. She'd pulled some cinnamon rolls out of the freezer, stuck them in the oven and set the table with her special Christmas china. It felt odd setting the table for three when for so many years it had been just her and Alex.

She peeked into the living room to catch another glimpse of Jake, asleep on the couch. Her breath caught. His legs hung off the cushions and he'd kicked the blankets off the couch, leaving only a pair of gym shorts covering his lower half. His face was smooth and expressionless in sleep, his profile silhouetted by the soft glow from the streetlight outside. Behind him rose the Christmas tree and three stockings hanging on the mantel. She'd hastily found another stocking last night so he'd have one too.

This morning, the stockings bulged with goodies from Santa. She happened to know the adult stockings held mainly candy, but Alex's also contained toys. Presents were stacked underneath the Christmas tree, brightly wrapped and ready to be torn open.

She smiled. Christmas was her favorite holiday. There was something magical about how it brought family and friends together to spend special times.

Her gaze returned to the man on her couch. He was both family and friend, and she suspected he would be a big part of her future. He looked like an angel sleeping there—an angel with a muscular chest and a six-pack of abs. She blushed, but couldn't tear her eyes away.

They'd been up late the night before, talking after Alex went to bed. He'd been through so much in his military career and had shared fascinating stories about the people and places he'd encountered over the years. It was a far cry from the life she lived in Candle Beach. But although she'd committed to live a nomadic life with Brian in support of his military career, a big part of her had always wanted to raise her children in her hometown. Jake opened one eye and caught her peeping at him. He smiled lazily and she blushed even more before scurrying into the kitchen.

He must think she was crazy, ogling him like that in his sleep. She heard him rise and dress as she busied herself in the kitchen.

"Good morning, beautiful." He came up behind her and kissed her on the neck. She smiled and felt herself melt against him.

"Good morning to you too." She kissed him lightly on the mouth and handed him a cup of coffee.

"Thanks, I needed this." He leaned against the wall and sipped the coffee. "We really pulled an all-nighter last night. I don't think I've been up that late since I was a newly minted Private."

"Sorry, it's been a while since I had another adult to talk to." She hung her head and hid behind her coffee cup.

"Don't apologize." He grinned. "I liked it. Made me feel young again."

"Oh yeah, the old geezer, pushing forty." She laughed and he tapped her on her shoulder with his knuckles.

"Hey, I resemble that," he quipped.

"Who's an old geezer?" a child's voice asked. Alex's dark hair stuck out in all directions as he rubbed sleep from his eyes.

"Uncle Jake." Maggie hugged her son. "Merry Christmas, sweetie. Are you ready to see what Santa brought you?"

Alex nodded vigorously and skipped over to the tree. He picked up a present and read the tag. "This one's for you, Mom." He handed it to her. He picked up another and gave it to Jake. Then his face lit up when he read the tag on a tall present Maggie hadn't seen before. "And this one's for me!" He ripped into it.

They watched as he tore off the Frosty the Snowman wrapping paper to reveal a large Batman Lego set.

"Cool!" he shouted. His eyes were wide with excitement.

Jake helped him remove the remaining paper. "I found this for you last time I was in Portland. I thought you might like it."

"I love it!"

Maggie had to stop Alex from opening the package. "Let's wait until later so we don't lose the pieces in all this wrapping paper."

"Okay," he said. "Thanks, Uncle Jake! We can build it tonight."

She smiled at them. Jake looked as excited as Alex about the prospect of building the Lego set, and she felt a rush of love for him.

Then Jake's phone rang, and he answered it. "Hello?" His smile faltered. "Sure, I can come in later. No problem."

"What's wrong?" Maggie asked.

"The department wants me to come in for a short shift later today. Our office support called in sick and they need someone on dispatch." He shrugged. "I'm the lowest man on the totem pole, so I get the job."

Maggie's good mood faded at the reminder of Jake's job. She and Alex were getting rather attached to him. Could she handle it again if something happened to Jake? She'd been devastated after losing Brian and it had taken years to get over the trauma of his sudden death. Now she was involved with another man in a dangerous job.

"Mags?" She felt him search her face. "You okay? There are more presents to open."

She forced her lips into a smile for Alex's sake. "Of course. Let's get them opened."

Alex passed Jake the gift she'd bought him. She'd found a Seahawks jersey in Haven Shores for him after he'd mentioned feeling left out at the bar when everyone else was dressed in local sports garb.

"Do you like it?" She peered at him anxiously.

He hugged her. "I love it. I'll wear it for Sunday's game."

She relaxed her shoulders. Gift giving wasn't her forte and it had been a while since she'd picked something out for a man other than her father.

They finished unwrapping everything under the tree. She was disappointed to see he hadn't bought her a gift, but tried to tell herself it didn't matter. She was just happy to have him sharing in their family holiday.

She pulled the cinnamon rolls out of the oven where they'd been warming and set them on a plate.

Alex tried to grab one and she swatted his hand away.

"Not yet, I need to ice them." She spread cream cheese frosting over the tops of the baked goods, making sure to leave a little extra in the bowl, which she gave to Alex to lick.

"Yum." He cleaned up the bowl with his finger and she wrinkled her nose.

"Use a spoon!"

He laughed and joined Jake at the table.

Maggie looked at her men sitting at their tiny kitchen table. Somehow, the kitchen seemed warmer and fuller with Jake and Alex there, waiting for her to join them.

Jake patted the seat between them. "Sit down. I'll get you some coffee."

She shrugged and sat down. She could get used to being waited on.

Later, Alex disappeared into his bedroom to start building his new Lego creation and the adults settled on the couch with another cup of coffee.

Jake checked his watch. "I've got to get to work, but I have something for you first." He reached into his pocket and withdrew a small velvet-covered box.

"Maggie, I never realized how much I wanted a family until I was lucky enough to spend time with you and Alex. These last few weeks have been the greatest in my life. Thank you for giving me the opportunity to be a part of your family."

He stared into her eyes and her heart beat faster. What was in that box? He couldn't be proposing now, could he? Things had moved fast with them because of their long history, and while she could see herself marrying him in the future, she wasn't ready yet. What if something happened to him? She couldn't lose another husband.

She gulped and leapt off the couch. "I don't feel so good," she muttered incoherently. Tears streamed down her face as she ran away from the living room, intent on hiding in her bedroom.

A knock sounded on her closed bedroom door a few minutes later.

"Maggie? Are you okay? I didn't get a chance to give you your Christmas present."

She could hear him hovering on the other side of her door. "I'm fine."

"Can I come in? Are you sick?"

Why was she acting like this? Every time she let him get close, she ended up pushing him away again. But, she couldn't face him right now...not like this. "I'm fine. I'll call you later, okay?" she said through the closed door.

He sighed. "I have to get to work, but I'll stop by afterwards. I hope you feel better later."

She pulled back the curtain on her bedroom window and watched as he backed out of the driveway. Then she dried her tears and opened the door. He'd left the black velvet box on the coffee table.

For the next few hours, she furiously cleaned the apartment, doing her best to forget about his gift. Her parents would be over in the evening to exchange gifts and she wanted it to look nice. Alex popped his head out a few times for food, but was wrapped up in his new toys.

Eventually, she couldn't take it anymore. She stared at the present for a few minutes. It was a box. Why was she so afraid of it? Gingerly, she picked up the clamshell box and opened it.

Inside was a beautiful piece of diamond jewelry—not a ring, but a simple drop pendant. She loved it immediately. She let out the breath she didn't know she'd been holding and tried it on. She should have known it wasn't an engagement ring. That was silly to have thought it would be. But a bigger part of her than she would have thought felt saddened by her discovery. Had she wanted it to be a ring? Was she ready for it?

A quick glance at the clock on the wall told her Jake would be off his half shift by now. He hadn't called or stopped by on his way home, probably because she'd scared him off. She grabbed the velvet box and shouted to Alex to get ready to leave. He poked his head out of his room.

"What? Why are we going somewhere?" He wore a puzzled expression.

"I need to talk to Uncle Jake. Hurry up, get your shoes on. You can bring one of your new toys."

He shrugged and for once did what she asked.

At the B&B, Maggie stood on Jake's doorstep, rubbing her fingers on the etching of the necklace he had given her. She wanted to tell him she loved him, but was afraid if she waited any longer, she'd lose her nerve.

She knocked, but he didn't answer the door. His car was in the driveway in front of his room and the door wasn't completely latched. She pushed it open a bit, but hesitated when she heard his voice. He must have been on the phone and hadn't heard her knock. She felt like she was intruding a bit on his privacy since he didn't know she was there, but she didn't think he'd mind.

"I think she's coming to visit you later this week, Mom." She smiled. He was on the phone with his mother. She was about to alert him to her presence when she heard him say, "I don't know what I did wrong. I think she's mad at me for something. I gave her a Christmas gift and she ran away." He sighed and his voice sounded weary. "You know, I came up here because I'd promised Brian I'd take care of her if anything ever happened to him. But this is more than I expected."

Her eyes widened and she backed away from the door, closing it softly. She edged blindly back to her car and shut the door. Was Jake only interested in her out of a sense of duty to his brother? Was that all she and Alex were to him?

Alex piped up from the back seat. "Mom? Are we going in to visit Uncle Jake?"

"No." She buckled her seatbelt and backed out of the driveway. "He wasn't home."

"But his car was there." Alex shot her a puzzled look.

"He wasn't there," she said, with more force than she would have liked.

Alex shrunk back against his car seat. "Okay," he said sullenly and went back to his game.

She drove back to their apartment in a haze. How was this possible? She'd allowed herself to fall in love again and it had all been a charade.

When Jake called her twenty minutes later, she didn't answer. After several more unanswered calls, a knock sounded on her front door. She didn't answer and he knocked again.

"Maggie? Are you in there?"

Luckily, Alex was engrossed in his Lego building project in his room and didn't hear the knocking. Maggie sat on the couch, staring at the door. She knew she should open it and allow him to explain the conversation with his mother that she'd overheard, but she didn't think she could handle hearing him confirm what she already knew. The only reason he was interested in her was to fulfill a commitment he'd made to his brother.

19

*J*ake lifted his mug of beer and drained half of it in one long gulp.

Across from him at the booth at the Rusty Anchor, Dahlia's eyes widened. She exchanged glances with Garrett next to her.

"Whoa, bud, slow down." Garrett took a small sip of his own beer. "This is craft beer, you're not supposed to down it like it's a Coors Light."

Jake hung his head. "I don't know what's going on with Maggie. She won't talk to me at all." He looked hopefully at Dahlia. "Has she said anything to you?"

She smiled sadly. "Sorry. Maggie plays things pretty close to her chest. If something's wrong, it takes a while to pry it out of her."

His spirits plummeted even further and he drank the rest of the beer and held out his empty glass to the passing waitress. She nodded and dropped off a refill of the local craft beer he'd been drinking.

The frosty glass felt cold in his hands, further enhancing the numb feeling. He'd thought they really had something going. Sheesh, he'd even had dreams of marrying Maggie, not that he'd admit that to her friends. He felt Dahlia and Garrett's eyes on him.

He'd checked in at To Be Read the morning after Christmas to see if Dahlia had any clue about what was going on with Maggie. She'd invited him for drinks with her new husband that evening, and he'd accepted because he hadn't really wanted to be alone. Now, watching Dahlia and Garrett sitting close together on the bench seat across from him, practically finishing each other's sentences, he wondered if he'd made a mistake. It hurt seeing how happy they were together.

"Oh," Dahlia said, and then pressed her lips together in a firm line.

"What?" He leaned forward and set his drink on the table. "What is it? Did you think of something that could be bothering her?"

She squirmed on the seat and even Garrett gave her an odd look.

"Well, I remember last year around this time, she was acting strange. The week before Christmas was her and Brian's wedding anniversary and then spending Christmas without him really affected her. She once told me that although she loved the holidays, this time of year was extra hard for her. Could that be why she's acting oddly?" Her eyes met his.

"I don't know." He set his glass on the table.

He wasn't sure whether to be glad there was an explanation for her behavior or for it to further fuel his concern that Maggie wasn't over his brother's death yet. If she wasn't over Brian, he understood, but he needed to know if she wanted to explore a relationship with him. For the sake of his heart and hers, they couldn't keep going like this.

"You should talk to her, man," Garrett said. "I know Dahlia and I had some misunderstandings that threatened our relationship. We wasted so much time worrying about stupid things that we could have spent together."

"I would if I could." He left his unfinished beer on the table and pulled some cash out of his wallet. "I'll try again. Thanks, guys."

They nodded and he felt their eyes on him as he threw on his jacket and exited the building. Outside, he looked up the hill toward the Bluebonnet Café. Was she there right now?

~

He checked the lobby of the café to see if Maggie was working the hostess desk. She wasn't there. At this time of the evening, very few customers were present in the restaurant. He poked his head into the back kitchen area and a crabby-looking septuagenarian glared at him.

"You're not supposed to be back here."

"Sorry." He gave her what he hoped was a smile that would charm an elderly woman. "I was looking for Maggie. Is she in?"

Apparently he was off his game, because the woman just scowled at him in response.

Everyone in the kitchen looked tired. It was quiet as the staff cleaned and the space lacked the usual energetic vibe he'd encountered when he'd been there in the past with Maggie. A younger woman beckoned for him to enter the kitchen. She was rolling dough on the counter, but smiled to let him know he was welcome. Was this the famous Angel? He couldn't tell what color her hair was because it was wrapped up in a hair net, but she was friendlier than the older woman.

"Hi. Are you Jake?"

He nodded.

She removed her gloves and walked over to him, sticking out her hand. "I'm Angel. That's Velma over there." She motioned to the older woman. "I just started here last week. Maggie talks about you all the time though."

A *humph* sound came from Velma's direction. He ignored her and shook Angel's hand.

"Nice to meet you. I wondered when I'd have a chance to meet Maggie's lifesaving baker."

She blushed and retreated behind the counter.

He looked around the kitchen. "Is Maggie here? I've been looking all over for her."

Angel's lips turned downward. "Sorry, she left to go home already. She'll be back in the morning though. I'm just finishing up here myself. Maggie wants us to meet at five tomorrow morning for a marathon baking session. She's such a slave driver." She smiled to show she was joking.

"She left already?" Now what? He'd hoped to catch her at the café where she couldn't avoid him so easily. If she was at home, she probably wouldn't answer the door. He was starting to feel like a stalker, but he needed to get some answers from her.

"Yes," Velma interjected. "She needed to go home to her son." She shook her head. "That woman is always leaving at the most inopportune times." She motioned around the room. "Look how messy it is. She was supposed to stay until closing time. Now we're stuck with that incompetent assistant manager. Humph. Well, at least she's home with her son where she belongs. Why, when I had a young child at home, you wouldn't find me working somewhere out of the home. All these career women nowadays. They think they can have everything."

Angel stared at her as though she'd grown wings. Jake's jaw dropped open, but he quickly recovered. He may not be high on Maggie's list of favorite people right now, but he wasn't going to let anyone talk badly about her.

In calmly measured tones, he said, "Maggie is the finest woman and mother that I've ever met. She's done amazing things with her life after going through one of the worst things a person can experience. I'd appreciate it if you didn't talk about her that way."

Velma glared at him. His fists clenched and he felt anger boil up through his veins, but he pushed it down. As much as he'd like to take the older woman to task, as a member of the Candle Beach police department, he had to maintain a good image for the department.

"She went home," Velma said flatly, and left the room.

Angel and Jake watched her leave.

"I'm so sorry about that." Angel walked over to the sink to wash her hands and then regloved. "I don't know why she would have said that. In the week I've been here, Maggie has been the best boss I could possibly ask for. And she's always telling stories about Alex. I can tell she loves being a mother. I don't know what she's been through in the past, but she seems to be making being a career woman and a mother work for her."

He smiled at her. "Thanks. I appreciate the support."

"No problem. I can tell you're a good guy and you care about her." She laughed bitterly. "I've dated some real winners and I'd marry the first one who came to my rescue the way you just did for Maggie."

He chuckled a little. "I hope she feels the same way about me. She's come to mean a lot to me in the small amount of time we've been together." He turned to leave. "It was nice to meet you, Angel. I'll check to see if Maggie's home now."

She waved from her station and he left. In this day and age, he was surprised to meet anyone who still thought a woman couldn't work outside the home and be a good mother.

He drove to her house, hoping that she'd finally give in and talk to him.

He knocked on Maggie's door. Although there was a light on in her bedroom, no one answered the door. He waited a few minutes and then left. When she was ready to talk to him, she knew where to find him.

20

_M_aggie had dropped Alex off the night before at her parents' house so she could come in for the five o'clock morning shift with Angel. The younger woman was working out well at the café, but Maggie still needed to teach her how to make a few more of the café's signature pastries. And if they weren't ready early in the morning, her regular customers would not be happy.

Jake had stopped calling and coming by her apartment. She'd had a full day to cool down and she still wasn't sure how she felt about him. The news that he was only interested in her to fulfill a promise to her deceased husband had shocked her to the core, but he was still her son's uncle and she didn't want to come between him and Alex.

After a morning of rolling dough for cinnamon rolls and wrangling the staff, she took a well-deserved coffee break in her office. She was enjoying the luxury of time to stare off into space when her phone rang. It was Gretchen.

"Hey." Gretchen's voice was cheery and music to Maggie's ears after the long morning she'd had.

"Hey, yourself. What's up?"

"I have some news for you." Gretchen let the tension build.

"What?" Maggie couldn't help asking.

"You know the farmhouse property you liked so much? Well, I have some good news for you."

"You do?" The property had gone under contract almost two weeks before, and she wasn't sure she'd call that good news.

"The other buyer's offer fell through."

Gretchen's words slipped through Maggie's brain like water dripping down a staircase. She'd thought the farm property was out of the picture and had put it out of her mind.

"What does that mean?" A sliver of hope edged at her consciousness.

"It means you can put an offer in now. It's back on the market."

Maggie leaned back in her chair. On one hand, she was excited about the possibility of buying the property, but it had already caused her so much stress and with things with Jake up in the air and falling fast, she didn't know if she could handle going through that again.

"Can I think about it and let you know?"

"Sure," Gretchen said. "But keep in mind there could be other interested parties. If you're serious about it, we need to put an offer in ASAP."

"Got it. Thanks, Gretchen. I'll let you know by later this afternoon."

She hung up the phone and her eyes wandered around her office. Her legs twitched, wanting to get out of the tiny room. She pushed herself up from the chair and took her coat off the hook.

"I'm taking my lunch break," she called to her staff. They nodded to show they'd heard.

With everything going on, she wasn't hungry, but coffee sounded good. She stopped off at the espresso stand near the beach and ordered a grande latte. Her legs carried her down to the beach by muscle memory. In a few minutes, she was standing on the sand and wondering how she got there. This was where she always came to think—something she desperately needed today.

She perched on a beach log and slowly sipped the creamy coffee. Two weeks ago, she'd been devastated by the loss of the farm property, but buoyed by a budding romance with Jake. Now, things had turned about-face and she had another crack at her catering center, but she'd lost the guy. Amazing how fast things could change. She knew that all too well.

Was owning the barn and farmhouse in her future? She'd purchased the café using Brian's life insurance policy and worked hard to make it a success, taking it from a greasy spoon to a popular eating spot for locals and tourists. It was a legacy she hoped to pass down to Alex. Could she really put that at risk to pursue this new dream of hers?

She stared out at the waves. They crashed rhythmically on the shore, washing away any imperfections in the sand. The wind blew her hair back and she shivered before taking a sip of her hot drink. Most people flocked to the ocean beaches in the summer, but this was when she really enjoyed them. In the winter, she often had the beach to herself—a perfect place of solitude to reflect on things. Usually, when she had a problem, she could sit here and let the shifting sands melt away her concerns. But Jake's betrayal and the immense responsibility of taking on a new business venture were too big for the sands to sweep away.

She stood and breathed in the cool air, allowing herself some peace before returning to her busy life. She didn't want to lose Jake, but it seemed as though she already had. Now she needed to get up the courage to tell him things were over and somehow do it in a way that didn't make things awkward between Jake and Alex. That would be tricky.

She knew what she had to do about the farm property. Buying it just wasn't a smart move for her current situation. Her stomach churned at the realization, but her mind felt clearer as the decision jelled.

She stopped at the garbage can at the top of the beach access stairs and threw in the coffee cup, turning to stare one more time into the ocean's abyss. Things had to get better from here, right?

~

After work, Maggie stopped by Jake's room at the B&B. She exited her car, eyeing the door with trepidation. It was a far cry from the joy she'd experienced a few days before when she'd come over to tell him she loved him and was ready to move forward with their relationship.

Before she reached the door, it swung open. Jake stepped outside, a tentative smile on his face.

"Maggie. I didn't expect to see you." He held his hand out to her, but she didn't take it. He stopped on the step.

"I had some thinking to do."

He nodded. "And what did you decide?"

She took a deep breath. "I don't think this is going to work."

The color drained from his face and he looked as sad as she felt herself. "Can you tell me why? I thought everything was going great until you ran away from me. Was my gift choice that bad?" He laughed nervously.

She shook her head. "It wasn't your gift. It was a lovely gesture. Thank you."

Her heart pounded. This wasn't how things were supposed to go with him. She'd been so sure that he was the right person for her. That is, until she'd overheard those fateful words, "I promised Brian I'd take care of her." She reached up behind her neck to unclasp the silver necklace chain and held it up to him, but he waved it away.

"Keep it," he said gruffly. "I want you to have it."

He wasn't a bad person—after all, he'd kept the promise he'd made to his brother. The problem was that he didn't love her, and she needed that. All the caring in the world didn't mean anything if there wasn't love attached to it.

"I want things to stay the same between you and Alex." She looked directly into his eyes, which glistened with unshed tears. If he was only in it because of a strange sense of duty, why was it bothering him so much for her to end things? Did he feel that strong of a commitment to his promise?

"Of course." He reached for her shoulder. "Are you sure we can't work things out? I really thought there was something between us."

She shrank back. If he touched her, it would be over. She'd turn into a melting puddle of tears and she couldn't let him see her like that.

"Maggie." He hesitated. "Is it because of Brian? Are you not ready to date again?"

He didn't need to know why she'd broken things off. He was a good guy, and it seemed easier to agree with him.

She nodded, glanced at him tearfully and speed walked

back to her car. She could feel his eyes following her until she was down the street.

21

*J*ake retreated into his room, the small space closing in on him. He opened the back window for some air and sat on the queen-sized bed, staring at the blank television screen on the wall.

What had just happened? Things had been going well with Maggie, and even after she'd freaked out on Christmas Day he'd expected they'd be able to patch things up. Now, there didn't seem to be much hope of that ever happening. He loved his brother, but there wasn't any way he could compete with a dead man.

How was he going to stay in Candle Beach now? Memories of Maggie were everywhere in town. And it wasn't like he had anywhere else to go. He leaned down with his elbows on his knees and hung his head low. The town had started to grow on him. He'd just gotten settled here and didn't want to leave. But did he have a choice?

As if on cue, his cell phone rang, with the readout showing an unknown caller. He tapped the answer icon. "Hello?"

"Jake Price?"

"Yes, this is Jake."

"This is Adler Saymet from the United States Border Patrol. I'm calling about your application for a Border Patrol agent job in our Blaine, Washington office."

He sat up straight. "Yes, sir."

"The Senior Agent you interviewed with was very impressed with your skills and qualifications. We'd like to offer you the position. We need you up there immediately as we have a training class starting Wednesday of next week."

His thoughts tumbled over each other. His feelings were mixed. This could be the way out of Candle Beach that he needed, but was it what he wanted?

"Can I think about it?"

The man on the other end of the line laughed. "We have thousands of people applying for every opening we get. As I said before, the position starts immediately. Are you interested in the position or should we move on to the next person on the list?"

There wasn't much choice. He knew if he didn't take the job offer, he'd never get another chance.

"Yes. I'll be there." He took down the details and hung up. Then he flopped backwards on the bed. Well, it was done. He was leaving Candle Beach—and Maggie—behind. Before he could make a permanent move to Northern Washington, he needed to get some things in Portland straightened out, including clearing out his storage unit.

Most importantly, he needed to say goodbye to Alex. He knew Maggie planned to drive down the next day to visit his parents in Portland, so he'd do it then. It wouldn't be a forever goodbye, he'd only be five hours away when he started his new job, but it would be a major change in the relationship he'd cultivated with the boy over the last month. His stomach twinged. He didn't want to leave Alex, but as much as Maggie said she didn't want things to be awkward, he knew things would never be the same between Alex and him again.

He walked the mile distance to the police station and tendered his resignation to the police chief.

"I'm sorry to see you go. We don't often get candidates with as much experience as you have." Chief Lee looked at him with a keen eye. "Are you sure there isn't anything I can do to convince you to stay?"

Jake drew his lips into a thin line. "I'm sorry sir, but there isn't. Due to personal reasons, I don't feel I can stay in Candle Beach any longer."

"Does this have anything to do with a certain young lady?" The chief stared at him.

"It may," Jake admitted. "But things aren't working out with her the way I'd like."

"I understand." The chief clapped him on the back. "If you ever need anything, let me know. I'd be happy to provide a recommendation for you if you ever need one. In the short time you've been here, you've done excellent work."

"Thanks, I appreciate it. I'll miss everyone here too."

Jake left the police station and walked out to Main Street. If he was going to leave early the next morning, he needed to make his goodbyes now.

He pushed open the door to To Be Read. Dahlia was with a customer at the counter, but she waved at him to let him know she'd seen him. He ordered a drip black coffee from the espresso bar and perused the titles in the mystery section while he waited for her to be free.

"Hey." She tapped him on the arm. "How are things going with Maggie? Did you get everything worked out?" She stared at him expectantly.

"No." He breathed deeply. "Actually, she broke up with me. That's the reason I came by. I'm leaving town to take a job with the Border Patrol. I wanted to thank you and Garrett for being so welcoming. I've truly enjoyed being here in Candle Beach."

Dahlia's smile faded and her expression became puzzled. "Oh. I'm sorry to hear that. She hasn't said anything to Gretchen or me about there being any issues. Are you sure you didn't misunderstand her? I'd hate for you to leave here. I know she cares deeply about you."

He laughed harshly. "Oh yeah. She was quite clear." He pursed his lips. "The truth is, she's not over my brother." He sighed. "I understand her position, I just wish I'd known before I fell in love with her."

Dahlia's eyebrows rose and her mouth dropped open. Jake immediately realized what he'd said.

"I shouldn't have said that. I should have known she wasn't ready for anything serious. But she's so darn wonderful, I couldn't keep myself from falling for her."

She laughed. "I know the feeling. The same thing happened to me with Garrett. I didn't think I was ready for a relationship until it practically bit me on the rear."

"Well, in your case, Garrett wasn't attached to someone else." He put his hand on her arm for a moment. "Anyways. Thanks. I've appreciated your friendship."

His next stop was the property management company.

Gretchen looked up from her desk with surprise. "Jake. I didn't expect to see you."

"I'm only here for a minute. I wanted to tell you I was leaving town."

She cocked her head to the side. "Does Maggie know?"

"No. But I think she'll be relieved I'm going. She broke up with me about two hours ago."

Gretchen stood to hug him and then sat down on the edge of her desk. "I can't believe it. She seemed so happy."

"That's what I thought." He shrugged. "But I guess appearances are deceiving."

"She turned down the opportunity to buy the Sorensen farm too. She just called me about an hour ago."

He narrowed his eyes at her. "What do you mean? Did the prior offer fall through?"

She nodded. "It did. But Maggie said she couldn't risk everything to buy it. I was surprised. She seemed to really want it. Usually when Maggie wants something, she hangs onto it like a dog with a bone."

He smiled sadly. "I know. Her tenacity is one of the things that attracted me to her."

"Something's going on with her, but I don't know what. She's not talking—at least to me. Are you sure you have to leave?"

"The job I'd applied for before coming to Candle Beach came through. If I don't take it now, it won't be there waiting for me." He looked ruefully at her. "I can't stay in Candle Beach, not without Maggie."

"I understand. I'll let Maggie know, okay?" She glanced at him with concern. "Did you tell Alex yet? He's going to miss you."

"I'm heading down to Portland tomorrow morning to see my parents and collect some of my belongings. Maggie said she was bringing Alex down there too, so I'll see him then. Probably good to see him on neutral territory."

She hugged him again. "We'll miss you. Good luck with your new job."

"Thanks." He left the office and walked aimlessly down Main Street. Across the street, children were playing on the swings in the grassy park next to the town square. He'd planned to put down roots and spend the rest of his life in this idyllic town. When he first arrived, he'd doubted the town's charms would affect him, but he'd grown to love the place in the short time he'd lived there. Now it would be just another place he'd lived temporarily.

~

Maggie threw herself into her work to forget about Jake. She planned to take Alex down to Portland to visit his grandparents for a few days and she needed to get everything sorted out at the café before she left. Hiring Angel had made things easier, but she didn't yet have Bernadette's experience as Maggie's right-hand woman, so she'd had to string together a team to manage the place in her absence. Luckily, she'd gotten the schedule finalized and everything seemed to have fallen into place.

That was, until Velma cornered her next to the schedule hanging on the café's kitchen wall.

"I just saw the schedule for Sunday." She stabbed at the paper with a gnarled finger tipped with red fingernail polish. "I told you I can't work Sunday mornings. I have church."

Maggie took a deep breath. "I know. That's why I didn't schedule you for Sunday morning."

"But you did." The old lady put her hands on hips and glared at her.

Maggie ran her finger along the schedule for the next week. Shoot. Velma was right. Somehow, she'd switched Velma and Denise on the chart and now Velma was slotted in for the Sunday morning shift. Normally, she'd never have made that type of mistake. It reinforced her decision to break things off with Jake and forget about the catering center for now. With so many balls in the air at all times, she couldn't afford to let any of them drop.

"I'll work with Denise to figure it out. I'm sure she won't mind. She likes to have evenings off."

"I never should have been on the schedule for that day." Velma glared at her. "I've been working here for twenty years and it never happened when Gus owned the place."

"I'm sorry. It was an accident and I'll fix it." Maggie smiled at the older woman through gritted teeth. Their conversation had been overheard by half the kitchen staff, who now watched the exchange with curiosity.

"Too many problems around here nowadays if you ask me," Velma said under her breath.

Maggie'd had enough. "Nobody asked you."

Velma recoiled as though she'd been shot. "Excuse me?"

"You heard me correctly the first time. Please don't pretend like you didn't. If you don't like how I run the café, you're welcome to leave. I'd hate to see you go because we appreciate your experience, but if you aren't happy here, don't feel obligated to stay." She held her breath.

Velma stared at her with eyes as big as silver dollars. "Well, I never." She stormed out of the kitchen.

The kitchen staff clapped and cheered.

"Good job, Maggie."

"I've been waiting for you to tell her off."

Maggie blushed and nodded at them before retreating to her office and firmly closing the door. What had she just done? She'd never lost her cool with an employee before, but Velma got under her skin. Thank goodness she was going away to visit her in-laws for a few days. She needed the time away from the café and everyone else in Candle Beach. An adult trip to the Bahamas would have been preferable, but she was happy for the chance to spend some time with Alex too. It had been a while since they'd spent quality time with just the two of them, something she planned to rectify while they were on vacation.

∾

Jake woke the next morning feeling slightly queasy but eager to move on with his life. He packed his meager belongings into his car and checked out of the room that had been his home for the last month. Driving along Main Street, he saw Lu's Chinese Restaurant, with its brightly colored red curtains and a gold cat in the window. Had it really only been a week since he'd been there with Maggie? That evening had started out so well, but had turned rocky. But she'd come back to him after that and their relationship had been stronger.

He passed by Candle Beach Kids and remembered his first full day in town, when he'd purchased the magnetic set for Alex—and how he'd felt an even stronger magnetic pull toward Maggie when they'd experimented with the toy. That had been the day he realized he had feelings for her that extended past physical attraction.

He had to get out of this town. Every store he saw, every person he saw, held some memory of Maggie. He'd made the right decision to take the Border Patrol job, even if it had its own downfalls.

When he stopped in Centralia to eat and make a pit stop, he checked his phone. Someone had called six times and left five voicemails. Maggie. Why did she need to talk to him so badly? He thought she'd have been happy to see him go. He pressed the buttons to listen to her messages and immediately turned his car around.

22

*M*aggie dialed Jake for what seemed the umpteenth time. Finally, he answered.

"Alex is missing. Is he with you?" she asked frantically.

"Slow down. You were crying so hard that I could barely understand your phone messages. What do you mean he's missing?" Jake's voice was low and soothing and Maggie felt herself relax. She usually considered herself good in a crisis, but all of that went out the window when the emergency situation involved her child.

"I woke up this morning and he wasn't in his bed." She sobbed and swiped at her nose. She'd already told the details to the police about twenty times. "I thought maybe he was hiding somewhere in the apartment, but I scoured the place and he wasn't there. It's not that big of an apartment. He's never gone out by himself before."

"Okay, calm down. I'm sure he's fine. Did he seem upset yesterday? I was on my way to Portland, but I'm coming back. I'll be there in about an hour and half—an hour if I break some speed laws."

She took a deep breath. "It's my fault. I told him about us

breaking up. Jake...he was so upset. He cried himself to sleep last night. I told him everything would stay the same between you and him, but he knew as well as we do that things would change."

"Did he leave a note or anything?" Jake's voice was crackly and she knew he was about to drop off in the cell phone dead zone on the way to the coast. His next words faded in and out and she couldn't understand them. She hung up the phone, clutching it in her hand like a lifeline.

She felt useless. The police had told her to stay at the apartment in case Alex came back, but it drove her nuts to not be doing anything to help find her son. She stalked into the kitchen and grabbed a sponge, attacking even the smallest specks of dirt as she mentally replayed the day's events.

They'd sent out the few officers in town to the houses of her son's friends and she'd called her parents and anyone else she could think of. No one had seen him. The apartment door was unlocked and she knew she'd locked it the night before. In light of how upset he'd been after she'd broken the news about her and Jake, she was sure he'd left on his own and hadn't been kidnapped. The problem was, he was six years old and the temperature was hovering just above freezing. They needed to find him as quickly as possible.

~

When Jake arrived, he sought out all the information he could about the situation, hoping for any clue that would help them find Alex. Chief Lee was in his office, directing the search efforts.

"Anything yet, sir?" In all his years in the Army and all

the hairy situations he'd found himself in, nothing compared to the terror he felt at the news that his nephew was missing in the dead of winter.

"Sorry, Jake. We haven't seen any sign of him. He's a smart kid though. Last time I saw him, he was showing off some magnetic science kit to me." He smiled and shook his head. "Always asking questions about things. He'll be okay. Don't worry. We'll find him."

Jake nodded and smiled slightly. "I gave him that kit. I know he's smart, but he's only a little kid. He has no idea what it's like to be outside overnight in freezing weather conditions." He looked at the clock. At this time of year, they had about four hours remaining until the sun went down. "I just stopped by to check on how things were going. I'm going to head on out to Maggie's place now."

He exited the police station and jogged back to his car. His mind raced with questions. Where was his nephew? What could have possessed the kid to take off like that? And how long could he survive outside by himself? He hoped Alex had been thinking straight enough to have worn his winter coat when he left.

He pulled up to Maggie's apartment and she ran out the door, not wearing a coat. She fell into him and he wrapped his arms around her. She shivered in her thin dress and he didn't release his hold on her until she was safely inside the warm apartment.

Her red curls hung limply over her shoulders and she hadn't put on any makeup. He brushed her hair back and led her over to the sofa. She collapsed into the cushions.

"He's gone, Jake. My baby's gone. And it's all my fault."

"Oh honey, it's not your fault. You told him the truth. You can't hide things like that from a kid like Alex. He's too smart." He felt helpless watching her dissolve in front of him.

She kept blubbering. "I shouldn't have told him until we were down in Portland. I knew it was a bad idea, but he wanted to know why I was so sad."

He stared at her. It wasn't the best of times to discuss their breakup, but he had to know. "You were sad? I thought this was what you wanted."

She looked deep into his eyes. "I never wanted to break up with you, but I knew it wouldn't work in the long term."

He didn't know what to say. The closet by the front door caught his eye. "Did Alex take his coat?"

She nodded. "That's how I knew he'd gone outside. I hunted all over the apartment for him, then checked the coat closet and saw it was missing."

At least Alex had something warm to wear. Jake stared at the closet where Alex hung up his jacket and backpack every day after school. The image of a colorful backpack leaning against a fence rushed to the forefront of his mind.

"Maggie. You said Alex took his jacket, but did he take his backpack too?"

"I don't know. It wasn't a school day, so I never thought to check." She rushed over to the closet. The spot where he usually hung his backpack was empty.

He put his hand on her shoulder. "I might know where he is."

"Really?" Hope hung heavily in her words.

He nodded. "He showed me a spot where he and his friends like to hide near the school. I told him it was dangerous and he said he wouldn't go there anymore. But it doesn't hurt to check it out."

"Go," Maggie ordered. "I'll stay here in case he comes back."

Alex's school and the abandoned house were within walking distance, so he ran over there as fast as he'd ever run in a PT test while in the Army. He probably broke his personal best record for the half mile.

The sky had darkened and he could see his breath in the cool air. They needed to find Alex fast. The abandoned house stood in front of him, its cracking white paint and broken windows as uninviting to him now as they had been when Alex had shown him his friends' secret lair. To a little kid though, the place was probably dangerous and exciting.

He squeezed through the opening in the chain-link fence and pushed away a broken board from the back of the house to enter the torn-out kitchen. It was colder in the house than outside, if that was even possible. The air smelled musty and damp.

"Alex? Are you in here?" He paused to listen.

His ears perked up when he heard a sound from upstairs, further back in the house, but no one answered. From his job at the police department, he knew homeless people made their way up to Candle Beach once in a while, but there wasn't a huge problem with squatters this far out of a big city. It was most likely Alex or some other kid in the house. Still, he kept his guard up, ready to respond if the situation went south.

He climbed the stairs. They creaked with each step and he hoped they'd hold his weight. At the top of the stairs, he turned the corner and pushed open a partially closed door.

∽

The windows on this floor weren't boarded up and a small amount of daylight illuminated the room. Dust motes floated in the air and water had leaked onto the floor through the cracked window panes, creating dark circles below the window frames. His eyes adjusted to the light and he sighed with relief.

Alex sat in the corner of the room with his back against the wall, hugging his knees to his chest. He eyed his uncle. "What are you doing here?" he sneered. "I thought you left."

"The whole town has been looking for you all day." Jake crossed over to him and crouched down beside him. "Your mom is in a panic. When she woke up and you weren't there, she was very frightened." He looked him in the eye. "You scared me too." He put his hand on Alex's shoulder. "It's really cold in here. Can you tell me why you ran away from home?"

"I know it's cold. That's why I brought the blankets."

He pointed to a few lightweight afghans Jake recognized as being from Maggie's apartment. His backpack lay unzipped next to the blankets, revealing some packets of cheese crackers and a single-serving bottle of juice.

Alex shivered and pulled one of the crocheted blankets over him. He glared at Jake. "I would have been fine."

"Buddy, your mom is extremely worried." At that reminder, he texted Maggie to let her know Alex was safe and they'd be home soon.

"She doesn't care about me. You don't either. Nobody does."

Jake sighed and slid down onto the floor next to him. "Why would you say that?"

Tears pooled in the boy's eyes. "You and Mom aren't together anymore. I thought maybe you'd be my new dad."

"Oh, Alex." Jake squeezed him around the shoulders. "Even if your mom and I aren't together, it doesn't mean I won't be in your life anymore. I'm still your uncle, you know." He smiled at him.

Alex hiccupped. "But you left without saying goodbye."

Jake's heart dropped to his stomach. "I knew you and your mom would be down in Portland today, so I'd planned to take you out to the mall before I left for my new job. I thought maybe we could pick up a new Lego set to build together." He rubbed Alex's head. "I'd never have left without saying goodbye to you, okay?"

"Okay." He smiled weakly and looked at Jake. "Am I in trouble?"

Jake didn't know for sure, but he suspected Maggie would be happy enough just to have her son home.

"Nope." He stood and stuffed the blankets into the open backpack. "But let's get you home now before you worry your mom even more." He held out his hand to Alex, who took it and scrambled to his feet.

Jake guided his nephew out of the room and down the stairs. As they exited the crumbling house, he took a last look at it. It was lucky Alex had confided his favorite hiding spot to him, or this could have been much worse. Goose bumps traveled up his arms when he thought about what could have happened if Alex had spent a night alone in the freezing house. He shook his head. The boy was found and would soon be reunited with his mother.

～

Maggie ran out of the house as soon as she saw them coming up the sidewalk.

"Alex." She almost barreled them over as she pulled her son close, hugging him as tightly as she could.

He squirmed. "I'm sorry I ran away, Mom."

"It's okay." She stroked his hair. Nothing mattered

besides him being home. He hugged her back and burst into tears.

"Honey, what's wrong?"

"I don't want Jake to go away. I love him."

Her heart tore into pieces. She looked into Jake's deep blue eyes and he smiled at her, forever trapping her. Was it enough that he cared for her, even if he didn't reciprocate her feelings? He would be good for Alex to have in his life, but would it be good for her in the long term?

Jake reached out and wrapped his arms around both of them. She let the warmth of his embrace wash over her, content to enjoy having Alex home again and Jake back in her life, even if it wasn't forever.

23

"This is beautiful. It's a perfect place to spend New Year's Eve." Maggie admired the view of the ocean from the window of the house in Candle Beach that her in-laws had rented for a few days.

Barbara Price joined her at the window. "I know. I can't believe it was available on last-minute notice."

"Thanks again for coming. After Alex disappeared, it totally wiped me out. It means a lot to me that you and John came up to Candle Beach to spend time with us. I know you hadn't planned to make the trip."

Her mother-in-law put an arm around her waist. "No problem. We both had vacation days to use and it was about time we came up here to visit you instead of you visiting us." She gestured around the house. "Besides, who could say no to this?"

Maggie smiled. They'd rented one of the most beautiful vacation houses in Candle Beach. The two-story house was right on the cliff overlooking the ocean and was walking distance to town. The owners had decorated it in a fashion straight out of *Coastal Living*, with turquoise walls and comfortable beige and white furniture. She'd have to keep Alex away from the couches when he was eating, but it was worth it to get to experience the luxurious surroundings.

"Thanks for hosting New Year's Eve too. I know my parents were excited to be invited to a party here."

"Of course. It all came together so nicely. I'm glad to see your parents again. It's been a while."

"And most importantly, I needed a place to sleep," Jake joked as he came up behind them. "Maude gave my room away and I'm homeless now until I leave for my Border Patrol job."

Maggie's stomach twisted at the mention of his new job, but she tried to push it away. It wasn't really her business what he did, as long as it didn't adversely affect Alex.

"Well, we wouldn't want that." She tried to keep her tone light. "Can I interest anyone in a hors d'oeuvre?" She motioned to the trays of mini pizzas and salmon bites she and Barbara had prepared earlier.

"Yum." Jake popped one in his mouth and smiled at her. She felt her face flush and turned around. She knew he was trying to keep the situation light. After he'd come back when Alex disappeared, they'd decided the best thing for Alex was for them to remain friends. But she found it hard to do that when every bone in her body screamed for them to be more than friends. What was it about him that got to her so strongly?

"Mom!" Alex tugged on her shirt. "Both grandpas and I are going to play Candyland. Do you want to play too?"

She glanced at Jake again and then said, "Sure. I'll be there in a minute."

She managed to avoid Jake until late in the evening. Her dad and father-in-law were passed out on the couch and Alex had sandwiched himself in between them, engrossed in some cartoon on the television. The older women chatted companionably, passing the time until midnight.

Maggie stepped outside onto the wraparound deck and leaned against the railing. The weather was unseasonably warm and she wore only a light jacket. Below the house, the waves pounded on the beach, the roaring of the waves soothing her senses. It had been a busy year. Both her friends had fallen in love over the last year or so, and she had too. At least she'd thought she had. Even though she and Jake weren't meant as a couple, she hoped they eventually could find their way as friends.

The sliding glass door closed behind her and Jake joined her on the deck. She tried it out. "Hello, friend."

He winced and took a deep breath. Then he put his palms on the railing and straightened out his arms, as if gaining strength, and looked directly into her eyes.

"Maggie. I don't want to be friends with you."

She stepped back and stared at him. "But that's what we discussed. For Alex's sake, we need to stay friends."

"I want to give us another chance." He ran his hand through his hair. "Honestly, I'm not quite sure why you broke up with me in the first place. You said it was because of Brian, but you'd told me you were over him. Which is it? If you aren't over him, that's fine. I understand. But I need to know the truth."

He wanted to know the truth? Was he happy being in a sham relationship with her? He was taking the whole promise to his brother thing a little too far. Well, he wanted the truth. She took a deep breath and let the words spill out.

"The truth is that I went over to your room at the B&B on Christmas afternoon. I'd realized how silly I'd been acting and I wanted to tell you I was ready for something serious with you."

"I never saw you there." He stepped closer to her and reached his arm out.

"Yeah, because I overheard you telling your mom about the promise you'd made to Brian to take care of Alex and me." A wave of embarrassment flowed over her. She'd come so close that day to telling him she loved him. Now, being honest felt like the right thing to do, but it still stung.

"Oh." He dug his hands into his pockets and stared out at the inky black waves.

"Look, I appreciate what you're doing, trying to make good on your promise, but I don't need your pity. Alex and I are doing fine on our own." She looked at him defiantly. "We don't need you to swoop in and save us."

He held up his hands. "Maggie, you've got it all wrong." She gave him a pointed look and he hesitated. "Well, maybe that was partially it in the beginning. Mom said you had a lot going on and I thought I could help out with Alex and maybe get to know the both of you a little better. But I never expected to fall in love with you."

She searched his face. "You fell in love with me? It wasn't all some misguided sense of loyalty to Brian?"

"No, of course not. Did you really think that?" He sighed. "From the moment I came back to Candle Beach, I haven't been able to get you out of my mind. I want to be a part of your life—and Alex's too, of course." He reached for her again. This time, she allowed him to pull her close to his chest.

Every sense in her body was on high alert. She was so close she could smell his aftershave mingling with the salt air and feel his heart pounding under his thin cotton shirt. She wrapped her arms around his neck and looked into his eyes. "I'd like that."

He bent down and kissed her, long and sweet. She

closed her eyes and allowed the kiss to deepen. Having Alex disappear had been the most terrifying thing she'd ever gone through, but in his own way, he'd brought Jake back to them. If Jake hadn't turned around to come back and help look for Alex, she doubted they'd ever have cleared up the misunderstanding.

He pulled apart from her, breaking their embrace. Feeling puzzled, she looked into his eyes, which twinkled with mirth.

"I think we have an audience." He pointed to the sliding glass door behind them. Both sets of parents were watching them with huge smiles on their faces. Alex gave Jake a thumbs-up.

She blushed furiously, but Jake returned Alex's thumbs-up and waggled his eyebrows at her.

"Should we go back in?" He held his hand out to her. She took it, squeezing it tightly. She never wanted to let it go.

They walked to the door, their family parting to allow them entrance.

Her father-in-law clapped Jake on the shoulder. "It's about time, son."

Her mother clutched her arm. "I'm so happy for you," she whispered. "We really like him."

Maggie did too.

24

"*I*'m so glad we were all able to get together this week." Maggie slid into the big corner booth at Off the Vine. Charlotte, Dahlia, and Gretchen were already there. "I hope you don't mind, but I invited my new friend, Angel, to join us. She's new in town and I thought you all would like her."

"Of course." Gretchen raised her wine glass. "The more the merrier."

"I'm certainly glad I got to know you girls better," Dahlia said as she dug into an order of nachos.

"Me too. But enough sappiness. I'm hungry." Charlotte pointed at a menu item. "Do you want to share the hummus plate?"

Maggie nodded. Then Angel walked in through the door and scanned the room. Maggie waved at her to join them and a huge smile crossed her face.

"Hi," she said shyly as she approached the table.

"This is Angel, my new pastry chef," Maggie said. "Angel, this is Gretchen, Dahlia, and Charlotte." They each gave a little wave.

"Nice to meet you." Angel sat down at the end and folded her hands in front of her on the table.

"We usually share the appetizers and then pay for our own drinks," Dahlia said helpfully.

"Sounds good." Angel ordered a lime margarita and then looked at Maggie with concern. "How's Alex? I was so worried about him when they said at the café that he was missing."

"What?" her friends said in unison.

"Maggie! When was this? Why didn't you say anything to us?" Gretchen frowned at her.

She shrugged. "I didn't want to bother anyone. I knew everyone was enjoying the holiday, and there wasn't much you guys could do." She sighed. "It was so scary though. I woke up on the morning we were supposed to go to Portland to visit Barbara and John, and he was just gone." She shivered at the memory. "I never want to experience that again."

"Yeah, it was lucky Jake was there," piped up Angel.

"Wait, Jake is still in town?" Dahlia asked. "I thought he left for his new job."

"He did. But I called him when I realized Alex was missing and he turned right around."

"And he found Alex," Angel said. Maggie looked at her and she blushed. "Sorry, Maggie," she whispered.

Maggie smiled at her and patted her hand. "Don't worry about it. I'm sure everyone will hear all the details soon, so I might as well tell you girls—Jake and I are back together."

"It's about time." Dahlia sipped her drink. "He was so torn up about your breakup that I knew he cared about you."

"Yeah, no kidding. If you don't mind me asking, why'd

you break up with him in the first place? He's perfect for you." Gretchen peered at her.

Maggie shrugged. "It was all a big misunderstanding. We've worked things through now."

"Thank goodness," Charlotte said. "Every time I've seen you together, you both looked so happy, and Alex too."

"I know. He does make me happy. And I love how good he is with Alex." She felt a warm glow spread throughout her whole body when she thought about Jake. "I thought after Brian died that I'd never have the opportunity to experience love like this again."

Gretchen and Dahlia smiled knowingly and Charlotte looked at her with dreamy eyes.

"You've all found the perfect guy. When is it going to be my turn?" Charlotte sighed.

"You and me both." Angel clinked her glass against Charlotte's and they giggled.

"You'll find him before you know it." Maggie shook her head. "Do you think I ever thought my womanizer brother-in-law would be the right guy for me?"

They laughed.

"So, I have some news," Gretchen began. Maggie checked her finger for a ring, but saw none. "Parker and I met with an attorney and drew up a partnership agreement. Our new company, Coastal Realty, will be a reality in a few months. We're still trying to figure out where we'll have our offices, but we're really excited."

"Yay!" Charlotte said. "I'm so proud of both of you. You've really worked hard for this."

Gretchen beamed. They all toasted to "New beginnings in a New Year."

Maggie toasted along with the rest of them. She knew she should be happy because she and Jake were finally together, and she was, but something still felt like it was missing. So many of her friends had pursued new career opportunities in the last year or two and she kind of regretted not going after the catering center. She knew the Sorensen farm property was out of her price range, but it still stung to not pursue a new business venture there.

Angel noticed she was quiet. "Are you okay, Maggie?"

She forced a smile. "Yes, of course. I was just thinking about the future of the café. I'm glad you're there. I think you're an even better baker than I am. I can see we'll be very popular come the tourist season with your skills."

Angel puffed up a little. "Thanks, Maggie. I appreciate that. I wasn't sure about coming to Candle Beach, but you've really made me feel welcome."

"Well, you're welcome." Maggie laughed at the pun. She'd told Angel the truth. The younger woman was a better baker than she was and quite capable. Maggie knew the café would be in good hands if she chose to pursue the catering center as her next challenge—if the opportunity ever presented itself.

~

A week later, Jake called Maggie to invite her to join him for a picnic lunch. She looked out her apartment window and raised her eyebrows.

"A picnic? In this weather?" Alex had complained of the cold that morning and she'd sent him off to school with an extra sweatshirt under his jacket. While there might not be snow on the ground, the sky was gray and she definitely wouldn't describe it as typical picnic weather.

He laughed over the phone. "We've got a few more months of winter, might as well make the most of it."

"Okay then." She brightened. This could be fun, and it beat the laundry she'd planned to take care of before Alex got home from school. "Is there anything I can bring?"

"Nope. I've got everything taken care of. All I need is you."

She blushed, glad that he couldn't see her reaction. "I'll see you at noon then."

When he arrived, he held up a bandanna in front of her.

"I'm going to put this over your eyes before you get in the car. It's a secret picnic location and I don't want to spoil the surprise."

She stared at the covering dubiously. She wasn't big on surprises, but he smiled at her and she forgot all her misgivings.

They drove for about ten minutes, until she heard the tires crunch on a gravel road and then stop.

"Where are we?" Were they at a beach overlook? A trailhead into the woods? It felt odd to be so close to home, but have no clue where they were.

"Be patient," he chided as he led her to their destination.

Finally, he allowed her to take off the blindfold. She blinked her eyes a few times as they adjusted to the light.

The first thing she saw was Bluebonnet Lake shimmering in front of her, its blue-green waters and foliage highlighted by the sun peeking through the clouds.

"We're at the Sorensen farm." She turned in a semicircle. Sure enough, the barn was to her right and the cute yellow farmhouse was behind her. She still thought it would have made a nice location for an event center. Her stomach lurched when she saw there was a big 'Sold' sign crisscrossing the real estate sign at the top of the driveway.

She sighed. "I knew this place would sell quickly.

Someone will be able to make this place beautiful again. I just wish it could have been me."

He placed his hand on her arm and led her through the scrubby grass to the far side of the barn. An oil-fueled heat lamp stood near a table that faced the lake. It was set for two with wooden farm chairs on either side. A rose perched in a petite crystal vase in the center of the table. He ducked into the barn, retrieved a wicker picnic basket and gestured for her to sit.

With a flourish, he popped the cork on a bottle of champagne and poured some for her. She watched as the bubbles fizzed up and spilled over the top of the glass. He dabbed at it with a cloth napkin and then removed a selection of cheese, crackers, and grapes from the picnic basket.

"Is there anything you don't have in there?" She peered into the basket, happy to see he'd remembered to bring some brownies for dessert. She could get used to pampering like this.

"Nope." He grinned. "It's a magic basket."

"I almost believe you. This is all so magical." With the heat emanating from the lamp, she didn't even feel the cold. There was something wondrous about sitting there, looking out over the lake and being in the country setting, but still so close to home. She thought again about how great it would be to share the view with others if it were an events center. She shook her head. When the time was right, she'd find the perfect place for her and her new business.

"I love this farm. How'd you talk the new owners into letting you plan a picnic here?" She reached for a cracker and placed some brie on it.

"Oh, it was pretty easy. I know the new owner well."

"Really? Is it someone I know in town?" She looked at him with curiosity. Rumor was. the person who'd made the previous offer on the property had been from out of town, so she would be happy if someone local had purchased the place. The last thing she wanted was for someone to come in and tear everything down to build a McMansion vacation home.

"I'd say you know them well." He winked at her. "I put an offer in late last week and paid cash for it this morning at the escrow office in Haven Shores."

Her jaw dropped. "*You* bought it?" She scanned the farm again. "But you hate it here."

"No," he corrected her. "I never said I hated it. I worried that it would be too much work for you with everything else going on." He made a face at the barn. "And that barn needs a lot of work."

"But what are you going to do with it? I never thought of you as a farmer."

"I'm not. But I do need a place to live now that I've given up my lodging at the B&B. I can't sleep on people's couches for much longer. Besides, I've been a single guy in the Army for twenty years. I've built up a nice savings account. What better place to spend it than on my forever home?"

"Surely there could have been some place in town that would be a better fit for you." She daintily placed a grape in her mouth.

"Probably, but then there wouldn't be a space for you to hold the biggest events in Candle Beach." He raised his eyebrows at her and grinned.

Excitement bubbled up throughout her body like the champagne in the glass. "Do you mean it?"

"Of course. I knew how much it meant to you. I needed somewhere to live and you needed this space. It was an easy decision."

"Thank you, thank you." She stood and twirled around

to see the whole property at once. "This is so amazing." She felt him watching her. Surprisingly, he hadn't dug into the food.

"I can pay you rent," she said quickly as she sat down. The barn remodel would be expensive, but she should be able to swing it with a construction loan using her savings account as collateral. At least now the café wouldn't be at risk.

"We can talk about it later. Actually, I had something more important to ask you." His voice cracked and he stood from the table.

Her eyes followed his every move. "What do you mean?"

He came over to her side of the table with a little black velvet box. She had a feeling that this time it didn't contain a diamond necklace. Her pulse throbbed loudly in her ears and she felt like she couldn't breathe until she heard him say the words.

"I know we've only been together for a short time, but I've been around the block a time or two and nothing has ever felt this right before. I think about you all the time. There's nothing more I've ever wanted in my life than to wake up next to you every day and have the privilege of being a father figure to Alex."

She started crying and he took her hand while getting on one knee. He opened the box to reveal a glittering princess cut diamond ring.

"Maggie Price. Would you do me the honor of becoming my wife?"

The tears fell faster. "Yes, yes."

He placed the ring on her finger and kissed her firmly on the lips. She kept crying. Her life had changed so much in the last two months that she barely recognized it anymore.

"Don't cry, honey." He wiped away her tears and held her to him.

"I can't help it. I'm so happy," she said, her words muffled by his shirt. She tried to stop crying, but it was as though the five years she'd spent alone had all dissolved in that moment. When she recovered, he released her and sat back down across from her at the table.

"Thank goodness you said yes. I'd be rattling around in that house all by myself," he joked.

She mock glared at him and dried her tears on a linen napkin. "You'll be wishing you were alone after living with a six-year-old going on sixteen-year-old."

He moved his chair next to hers. "I'm looking forward to it."

He put his arm around her and hugged her to him. She slid over their joined seats to get closer to him, wrapped her left arm around his waist and rested her head and right hand on his chest.

They stared out at the lake together in contented silence. Her thoughts brimmed with visions of the big parties they'd cater and the times they'd share as a family there on the old Sorensen farm. Alex would play down at the lake and maybe there would be a brother or sister for him in the near future.

She realized she'd spoken that thought out loud when Jake said, "Oh definitely there will be a brother or sister. Maybe a couple of them."

She hugged him tighter. She'd thought she was perfectly happy before, but now she knew the best was yet to come.

<<<<>>>>

THANK YOU FOR READING SWEET PROMISES!

Want to spend more time in Candle Beach?

Dahlia's Story: Sweet Beginnings

Gretchen's Story: Sweet Success
Available on Amazon and Kindle Unlimited

I hope you enjoyed your stay in Candle Beach. I'm busy writing the fourth Candle Beach sweet romance and a new cozy mystery series also set in a small town. Please visit my website, NicoleEllisAuthor.com to stay up-to-date on my new releases.